A VACATION CRUISE TO ACAPULCO . . .

Setting her story on an oceangoing liner, Ms. Christian creates a floating microcosm of lesbians on a holiday voyage. Women from all walks of life meet each other for the first time aboard the S.S. *Sisterhood*, sharing experiences both sad and glad. . . .

Most of us will recognize the characters as people we've known . . . or even see facets of our own personalities. The passengers fairly leap from the pages as living, real people – with hopes and fears common to us all.

Come aboard and meet them . . . this is a novel you're not likely to soon forget!

Timely Books is proud to offer this long-awaited, new work of lesbian fiction by Ms. Christian. This outstanding first novel since 1965 is a definite publishing event, and we're joyfully christening it with champagne!

OTHER NOVELS BY PAULA CHRISTIAN

Edge of Twilight
This Side of Love
Another Kind of Love
Love Is Where You Find It
The Other Side of Desire
Amanda

PAULA
CHRISTIAN

THE CRUISE

timely books

p.o. box 267
new milford, connecticut 06776

DEDICATION

To women – one and all, everywhere

An original Timely Books publication.

First printing October 1982
Second printing December 1983

This is a work of fiction, and all characters and events are fictitious. Any resemblance to people, living or dead, is purely coincidental.

Library of Congress Card Catalog Number: 82-060183

ISBN 0-931328-09-8

Cover illustrated and designed by F.R. Vallone
Typesetting by Sister Media Typesetters

Timely Books
P.O. Box 267
New Milford, CT 06776

THE CRUISE

CHAPTER ONE

FELICE CAPEZIO LEANED on the railing of the S.S. *Sisterhood* and for the thousandth time, wondered if she'd done a stupid thing. In all her thirty-four years, she'd wanted to take a cruise to Acapulco; but she'd either been too young, too broke, or too shy. She was the only one of her set who had never been to Europe, and as a consequence, the butt of numerous unintentionally cruel jokes. Felice had always wanted to travel, yet the idea of doing so all alone didn't appeal to her. When friends jetted off to Paris or London or wherever, they went as couples, off to have a good time. Who needed a single tag-along? Certainly, on several occasions, she'd been asked to come too; but either she couldn't get away from her job at that time, or she felt that the invitation was extended in hopes she'd refuse – and she had.

Frequently, she'd thought of taking a cruise to Europe instead of flying. At least, aboard ship, she might meet some convivial people with whom to explore the shops and interesting sites of any ports they might put in. She'd been with Kloberg Publishing long enough – ten years – to be entitled to a three-week vacation, so it wasn't really out of the question. What stopped her were all the tales she'd heard about shipboard romances, the boy-meets-girl moon-June nonsense; cocktails, dancing to hopelessly outdated music, all of it. That was no place for Felice Capezio. It was no place for any dedicated, confirmed lesbian. Such vacations were for lonely librarians, or schoolteachers, looking for romance leading to marriage. Felice didn't want such things.

Or, at least, not heterosexually. It wouldn't be much fun to take a long ocean voyage with a bunch of people whose lifestyles were totally alien to hers. The misfit younger men, or the self-appointed Don Juans, would make a pitch for her; she'd back off, and inevitably, there'd come the question cum accusation: "What's the matter? Are you a queer?" It used to humiliate her, hurt her feelings terribly – but it no longer did. It was simply awkward. She'd learned, the hard way, that if you don't want to be considered "abnormal," don't hang around with the majority. Simple. Cliché or not, life was easier if you stuck to your own kind. While that certainly wasn't possible on her job, she did have the choice in her private life.

Then, when she saw the ad for the all-lesbian cruise aboard the S.S. *Sisterhood*, leaving from Los Angeles on December 20, it all began to fall into place. On impulse, she'd telephoned her best friend to kick the idea around.

"You're crazy!" Ann had said.

"Why?" Felice was quite accustomed to Ann's initial negative response to anything.

THE CRUISE

"Who knows what sort of women you'll be stuck with? And at Christmas yet! A bunch of lonely-heart lesbians – probably the California camper set! – all looking for their kicks on some stupid cruise. It's a crazy idea, Felice, forget it."

She'd smiled against the receiver. "I'll meet other women just like me, Ann. What's wrong with that?"

"Aw, c'mon. What kind of people would openly take a cruise that's one hundred percent lesbian? Militants, rub-it-in-their-faces lesbians. Not your sort of people at all. They'll have cigarette packages rolled up in their tee-shirt sleeves, say a lot of 'Hi, guy!' and all that camper argot. They'll talk about their dogs as if they were babies, the terrific CB just installed in their vans, the last time they camped out at the desert . . . oh please! No way!"

Ann was a copywriter for a leading New York advertising agency; she hated most people, especially the masses, but she knew how to reach them. "Look, Felice, I'm not joking. You go on that cruise and you'll end up playing shuffleboard with the 'guys,' and taking a crash course in Spanish with the fems. Some jerk will ask you to dance on New Year's Eve, and some diesel-dyke will crush your face for you. You're a nice person, chum; educated, refined, and acceptable in any strata. Why would you want to be confined with that other sort for a whole cruise?"

"But what if," Felice had answered, "I should meet someone I really liked. Someone who, like me, just wants to have a nice getaway with people you don't have to lie to? No games, no excuses, just fellow lesbians wanting to enjoy a pleasant vacation?"

"You won't. Believe me, you won't," Ann had said.

Felice had given a great deal of thought to Ann's advice. It was true, she'd be running a very large risk of having an absolutely grim time. Still, she cut out the ad and clipped it to her refrigerator door. With the gulped morning coffee, she would look at it; and every evening, preparing a solitary dinner, she'd reread it. She could either spend a week at home in New York, hoping it wouldn't snow so she could catch up with the dull details of her personal life; or spend the time in San Francisco or Los Angeles prior to sailing date. Then, on the cruise, dipping into sleepy Mexican ports until they reached Acapulco – the Riviera of the West. The more she considered the idea, the more she came to believe in its merits. An entire ship couldn't possibly be filled with nothing but sun-dried lesbians. It just wasn't logical. She'd meet someone; she could feel it. Some gracious woman who didn't hang around in gay bars, who didn't drool over Barbra Streisand or Judy Garland, who didn't think Humphrey Bogart imitations were cute, and who didn't wear jockey shorts and argyles – or no bra and no makeup.

Now, standing at the railing as the ship pulled away from the Wilmington docks south of Los Angeles proper, Felice hoped she had been right in her decision. Well-wishers crowded the edges of the dock, predominantly female; waving, catcalling, cheering, and very rowdy. If those were the friends of the passengers, Felice wondered, what would the passengers be like?

¤ ¤ ¤

Donna Cunningham wrapped a tanned arm around Sandy's waist as they peered through the porthole of their cabin four tiers beneath top deck. The evidence of a bon voyage party was all about them, but they ignored it as they waved to their friends on shore. "Can you believe it?" Donna asked. "We're finally going somewhere without the camper!"

Sandy smiled up at her, excitement glistening in her

pale blue eyes. "Are you sorry, Donna? Do you wish we'd taken the babies and gone to Tahoe instead?"

"Nah," Donna said, hugging the shorter woman to her. "You've got to have change in your life, or you get stuck and your whole life goes by before you know it. And don't worry about the kids, Sandy. Everyone we know says that's a great kennel. They'll be okay."

"I hope so, darling," Sandy replied, reflectively. "But you know Bojangles has had that sniffle, and Mutt gets so upset when we leave him anywhere."

Donna looked down at her, a happy grin on her face. "Are we going to have a good time, or are you going to worry?"

Sandy looked up at Donna, then threw her arms about her neck. "You know what's best, Donna, you always know!"

"That's right, and don't you forget it." She lowered her face to Sandy's, and kissed her tenderly. *She's such a kid*, Donna thought, then lost herself in their kiss.

Sandy's fingers began to work at Donna's shirt, and when their lips parted, her expression was downright lustful. "C'mon, we've never done it on a ship before."

Donna laughed, letting herself be led to the bunk bed. "No, but we did it in a canoe once, remember?"

The younger woman snuggled up to Donna on the bed, her legs pushing against Donna until one broke through to its target. "I don't care about where we've done it before, darling . . . I care about now . . . right now!"

Donna laughed, but she was deeply mindful of the pressure against her crotch. "You're the hottest taco in the West, Sandy!"

¤ ¤ ¤

THE CRUISE

Erika Schultz squinted cautiously at Charlene McCambridge and watched the woman as she methodically mapped out her personal territory in the cabin: jewelry cases on the right-hand side of the built-in bureau; neatly rolled pantyhose, bras carefully folded, half slips, scarves, white gloves, and her horrendously garish, expensive diamond ring in its own velours box – all in the top right-hand drawer.

Charlene moved with cumbersome purposefulness, as if to do anything quickly would destroy her chain of thought. She moved with slow deliberation from the open suitcase on the right-hand bunk bed to her planned destination with the right-hand drawers. What had always amazed Erika about Charlene was that the woman was left-handed; why she had this compulsive bit about the right eluded Erika.

She watched the stocky woman's movements half in amusement and half in derisive resentment. *I'll kill her one of these days*, Erika thought with no hint of assertive violence in her soul. *I almost have to – if I'm ever going to be free of her.*

"Why aren't you unpacking?" Charlene asked as she took six neatly folded blouses – blouson style to hide her middle-age lack of waistline – and placed them in the second drawer.

"I will."

"When? After the cruise is over? When you're back home again? My God! I don't know how you managed to exist all those years without me. You've got to be forced to do *any*thing! You're like a child, Erika. If you're not told what to do, you just stare into space doing nothing."

Erika leaned against the wall, crossing one leg in front of the other, and grinned. "Is that it for now? Or are you just winding up for the real thing?"

Charlene shot her a dirty look. "What about those new cashmere pants I bought you at Brooks Brothers? You just going to let them get all wrinkled so you can look like yesterday's newspaper? They were damned expensive, Erika, and the least you could do is hang them up!"

Erika sighed, leaned over and lifted her suitcase onto her bed. *She's winding up, here we go again!* They'd been lovers once – how many years ago? – and now they were enemies who shared the same abode, the same routine; but like strangers, each going her own way. *No*, Erika thought, *Charlene gets to go her own way – I'm not allowed. I'm chattel. Totally dependent on Charlene for every morsel of food, shelter, and the fuckin' clothes on my back. I hate her so goddamn much it's funny. And I'm stuck. Oh wow, but am I ever stuck!*

". . . And I don't want to see you hanging around the swimming pool, either, y'hear? This trip is costing me a fortune, Erika, and you're here to work . . . not lollygag or ogle all the young fems aboard this floating crate!"

"Get off my back, Charlene," she said casually. "I'm chaste as a nun in solitary. Gave up sex, remember? It's counterproductive."

The stocky woman snorted. "If I didn't watch you every second, you'd bed everything from here to Peoria like the plague sweeps the land."

Erika laughed. "Good imagery. You should be the writer, not me."

"Well, I'm not, and don't forget it. I'm your agent, dammit, and you're going to finish that book during this trip or I'll kick you so far out you'll be in perpetual orbit!"

"I'll finish it, I'll finish it! Will you knock it off?"

"You're two months behind deadline right now, do you realize that? How long do you think people are going to care about all these way-out religious fanatics? The market's going to drop out on us, and I'll lose plenty. I've my reputation with publishers to think about, too! I give them a hard-sell pitch, get you a hefty advance against royalties, and you fail to deliver. Really, Erika, sometimes I think you do these things on purpose, just to embarrass me."

Erika counted to ten, keenly aware of her temples throbbing. It took everything she had to try to sound calm and reasonable. "Writing about these cults isn't something you can do easily, Charlene. They're all sharp, and used to a lot of bad press – they're not going to open up to any stranger all that easily. As for the advance, you kept it, remember? Said I owed it to you for my share of the rent?"

"I gave you some of it," Charlene said, the trace of a whine in her voice. "After all, I've been supporting you for over three years, and that's the first money you've made in almost five years! I don't have to support you, y'know! We're not exactly husband and wife!"

Erika didn't bother to retort that five hundred dollars out of a five-thousand dollar advance wasn't exactly riches. And what galled her the most was that Charlene was right; without Charlene's aid, she'd have been on the streets long ago. Win, lose, or draw, there was no way in hell to get rid of Charlene short of jumping off a bridge – or killing the broad!

¤ ¤ ¤

She stepped back from the mirror tilting her portable makeup lights for maximum efficiency and glaring truth. The first three layers of her makeup had been applied, but she still had about another forty minutes' worth of application before she'd be through. There was the contouring yet to be done, shading, eyelashes to be glued, and she still had to carefully comb her shoulder-length ash-blonde hair for that casual, wavy look. Lynn Adler earned two hundred dollars an hour as a high-fashion model and she lived the role sixty minutes an hour, twenty-four hours a day. Her parents, who were both successful attorneys in California's fashionable Laguna Beach, had given her the benefit of an expensive education, yet she had spurned the idea of a professional life. Lynn wanted adulation . . . even if she never met any of her admirers, she wanted to know that men looked at her and wanted to bed her; and that women would lick their lips at the sight of her.

For as long as Lynn Adler could remember, her mother had admonished her that she'd only be young once, so enjoy it. And Lynn could think of no better way to enjoy her youth than to be sought out, adored, even revered. She reveled in it. There was never any doubt in her mind that she'd refuse to spend her youth with a bunch of dreary textbooks, studying for an M.A. or Ph.D. for some dull career. She'd worry about a profession later, when she was old . . . at thirty, or maybe thirty-five. But for now, she wanted to enjoy what her looks did to people; turn them to putty. That was power, real power. Male millionaires offered her anything just for a date. Their wives were smarter; they sent the expensive presents to her first, then suggested dinner somewhere out of the way. Maybe they had more money than she, but they didn't have the power she had, and Lynn basked in it.

Beneath all the makeup, Lynn had good, regular features, but she was no beauty. With the makeup, the right designer clothes, and the tracking spotlights on her while she walked, dipped, or whirled on fashion runways . . . she was deliciously beautiful. And she knew it.

The phone in her cabin rang, and she was so startled that her hand jumped and she wrecked the slight curve of the eyeliner. "Goddamnsonofabitch!" she muttered, tossing down the thin brush. She crossed over to the phone of her double-occupancy cabin – Lynn knew she'd need the space when those horny fools got a look at her – and jerked the receiver off the hook. "Yes?" she drawled out sweetly.

THE CRUISE

"Ms. Adler?" The woman's voice was deep, almost husky.

"Yes, this is she," Lynn answered, maintaining the same surprised and oh-so-interested tone.

"I'm Carmen Navasky, the coordinator for this cruise."

"Yes?"

"I, uh, well, I'm pulling together the dining room assignments, and, uh, I thought you might like to be included on the list to sit with the ship's captain."

"That would be just lovely," Lynn said, a smug smirk on her face. If this Carmen Whateverhernameis was the same woman she'd seen when she'd boarded the ship, she'd been positively drooling at the sight of Lynn. And Lynn was certain that – just somehow, mind you – Carmen Whatsherface would also just happen to be seated at the captain's table. . . .

"Yes, well, I'm sure you realize that it's considered quite an honor."

"Well, isn't that sweet of you to think of me."

The woman cleared her throat nervously. "The, uh, captain prefers to have his dinner at the second seating, Ms. Adler. Is seven o'clock convenient for you?"

"Of course!" Lynn answered with studied childlike glee. "Whatever you say is just fine with me."

"Good. Then, I'll put your name down for seven, at the captain's table."

"Thanks so much, Miss – ?"

"Navasky," the woman offered again hastily. "But I was wondering if – if you're not otherwise engaged, that is – if you'd care to join me for a cocktail before dinner?"

Lynn turned the invitation over in her mind swiftly, weighing how it might affect her standing during the rest of the voyage. How smart would it be to be seen, their first night out, with the cruise coordinator? It might look as if the two of them were an item, and that wouldn't do.

Obviously sensing something amiss, the woman added: "It won't be just the two of us," she said quickly, as if she had already planned a backup story. "Several of the other passengers will be at the lounge. It's just sort of a getting-to-know-you drink, break the ice, that sort of thing thing."

"I see," Lynn offered cautiously. "At what time?"

"Six. At the Neptune Lounge on the promenade. That way, we can all watch the sunset and relax a little before dinner."

Lynn was confident that this woman would now have to dig up several other passengers to join them, that it hadn't been her initial intent. "I think that would be lovely," she said after a moment. "It's so nice of you to include me."

"Not at all, Ms. Adler, not at all. Six o'clock, then?"

"I'll be there," Lynn answered airily, then hung up. She went back to her mirror, all smiles, and tingling with anticipation. It had begun. That same thrill of being a prize to others; hunted, pursued, lusted after. Her loins ached as she envisioned the mouth-gaping stares of all those women when she entered the Neptune Lounge.

Lynn gazed lovingly at her reflection in the mirror. "It won't be just the two of us," she mimicked. "You bet your sweet ass it won't! Not with a whole boatload of women trying to get in my pants . . . I'll take my own time deciding which of them is going to get lucky!"

CHAPTER TWO

THE PROMENADE DECK of the S.S. *Sisterhood* was a treasure of Art Deco. In its day, it must have been quite a luxury liner, but now, fifty years later, the signs of wear and tear couldn't be fully camouflaged. The flowing, rounded moldings along the walls of the Neptune Lounge showed chips and occasionally, the telltale peeling of cream-colored paint. The frosted glass chandeliers, in the shape of huge pears – complete with stems and leaves – seemed archaic. One could've considered it high camp, had the ship been recently refurbished in that decor; but the fact that it was the original, neglected over the years, made it pathetic; like an old woman, wearing the makeup and clothes of her youth, trying to pass for twenty again –

or still.

However, Carmen Navasky wasn't worried about it. This was the maiden voyage, a relatively new concept in the travel business. There were a few other travel agencies offering all-gay tours, but Carmen doubted that any could match this cruise to Acapulco. Their voyage would take them all the way down to the tip of Baja California, putting in at Mazatlán on the mainland, then Puerto Vallarta – popularized by the torrid romance between Richard Burton and Liz Taylor – then on down to lush Acapulco in the state of Guerrero, on the Pacific side of Mexico. A perfect cruise for sun-loving lesbians, with no dirty looks or sneers from the straight crowd.

There'd be a lot of hanky-panky, Carmen knew, and they would have to be on the watchout for possible jealous rows between lovers – but good God! that happened on any cruise, regardless of the sexual orientation of the passengers. Sometimes Carmen wondered why she stayed in the business; dealing with the public was a thankless world that would render even a cretin to a basket case. Small tours weren't quite so bad. If you were only dealing with ten or twelve people, the chances of being able to reason with them were much greater. But in the hundreds, it was an impossibility.

She smiled to herself as she scanned the lounge, making certain there was a fresh flower on each of the tables. The lavender tablecloths had been a nice touch, she thought, and Carmen glanced at her watch. Five-fifty-five. She tried to guess if Lynn Adler was the punctual type; probably not, she decided. With her looks, she could be anything she damned well pleased and get away with it. She was so beautiful that Carmen couldn't help questioning why the girl would be gay. *And that's really conditioned thinking*, Carmen chastised herself. *Since when has beauty had anything to do with it?*

She glanced over at the bartender, a burly woman absently wiping glasses, checking setups behind the bar. Bernice Wellington was either a victim of genetics or a one-woman psychological backlash. She was known as Bernie to everyone, and anyone attempting to call her Bernice was likely to find herself thrown out a door. Bernie was more than butch; she was a man; more of a man than a lot of men around. She'd tended bar in gay clubs all her life. Affable with the customers unless they got out of line; if that happened, Bernie made Man-Mountain Dean look like a ballerina.

Carmen had had a "twenty-minute" fling with her once, years and years ago. She'd been quite young, then, and more than a little drunk. Though she knew she was gay, she'd never had any physical experiences. When Bernie put the make on her, Carmen had been terrified to the core, but too curious to let the opportunity go. For Bernie, it was instant love; for Carmen, it was a crash course in Introductory Lesbianism.

But she'd let Bernie down gently, and there'd been no hard feelings or hostility. It was the name of the game. Hanging around with fresh meat was to risk it going rancid. Bernie had understood. Though they never socialized, Carmen was always quick to recommend Bernie for any bartending gig she might hear about, and Bernie was appreciative. There weren't an awful lot of places for card-carrying dykes to get jobs back in the 1950s and '60s.

Carmen checked her watch again. Five-fifty-eight. Any moment now, Lynn Adler could be walking through the door and Carmen only hoped she'd be able to keep her cool, not just babble inanely. Well, thank God she'd been able to round up those other women to join them. She'd checked the passenger list carefully, and hoped the mix would be a good one. Felice Capezio was in the publishing business in New York; there was that agent, something McCambridge . . . Charlene! yes that was her first name; and the agent's roommate was a writer, so that was good.

Carmen was only a little worried about the other two. Donna Cunningham was a parole officer in Los Angeles, and her roommate was a high school gym teacher. Not exactly the literary or jet set, but what the heck, there had to be a balance if this little social gathering was to be a success.

Six-o-five. The door to the lounge pushed open slowly. Carmen turned expectantly.

"Am I in the right place?" Felice Capezio asked.

Carmen smiled graciously. "Yes, you're merely the first one to arrive. Hi, I'm Carmen Navasky."

Felice entered the room, her curly dark brown hair carefully coiffed in a short style to frame her attractive, oval face. "I'm afraid I'm just a little late," Felice said, a faint smile on her lips. "I'm fascinated by the boat's decor!"

"Don't let the crew hear you call their ship a 'boat.' They get very uptight about that sort of thing."

"Really?" Felice stood in the middle of the room, taking it all in. "I'll try to remember that," she said, her dark brown eyes revealing amusement at her faux pas.

Carmen gazed at the woman, aware of Felice's good figure and excellent taste in clothes. But it was easy to see she wasn't one of the A-List, not part of the inner circle of chic and successful women. Though she had poise, it was rather uncertain; she dressed well, but not designer clothes; and Carmen was confident, even at a short distance, that her jewelry was electroplated gold, not real. Pity. Attractive enough, but something was missing – probably money.

The lounge door was thrown open abruptly as Donna Cunningham held it open for Sandy Wohl. Actually, they'd signed the register in the lobby as Donna and Sandy Cunningham, but the law required Sandy to also provide her "maiden" name. They wore identical wedding bands, and entered the room like cooing lovebirds.

"Hi," Donna boomed, thrusting her lean hand toward

Felice. "Nice meeting you, Ms. Navasky."

"I'm Felice Capezio," she said, then gestured to her right. "She's Carmen Navasky."

"Oh, well, nice to meet you anyhow," Donna said. "This here's Sandy, the little woman."

Carmen's face remained a pleasant hostess-like mask but she didn't fail to notice that Felice seemed somewhat shocked. "Welcome, welcome," Carmen said, coming forward to shake their hands. "How about a drink, ladies?"

"You call 'em, I'll mix 'em," Bernie said from the bar, her stubby hands spread open on the highly polished surface.

"Umm, a daiquiri for me, I think," Felice said, making her way toward the bar, feeling quite out of place and awkward.

"Hell, I'll have a beer! What kind you got?" Donna asked.

"Name it," Bernie said.

"Coors." Donna twisted and glanced back at Sandy. "What about you, doll? What's your poison?"

"Whatever you're having, Donna." Sandy pulled back a chair from a nearby table and fell onto it as if all her joints had come out of their sockets. "Whew! Sure is warm today, isn't it?"

Carmen laughed. "Wait! It'll get a lot hotter."

"Hey! Don't pour that beer in a glass. Just hand us the bottles!"

"Name's Bernie," the bartender said without expression.

"Yes, by all means, you should meet Bernie. She'll be your bartender every night of the cruise. And there's not a drink invented she can't mix," Carmen interjected.

"Hi," Donna said, sticking her hand out. "Seem to think you and me've met somewhere else before. Ever work in a joint called Marjie's up in Atascadero?"

"Nope."

"Well, I'll think of it, come one of these days. But I know you and me have met each other somewhere."

"I've worked the whole country, guy – even Hawaii."

"Been in the service?"

"Nope. Tried, though. During Korea. The WACS wouldn't have me. Got as far as the physical with the men's branch, but without a dick, I couldn't get in."

"Yeah, know what you mean," Sandy said sympathetically. "Donna tried to enlist too."

"Which branch?" Bernie asked, almost indifferently.

"Marine Corps," Donna said, a scowl crossing her face as if it still pained her to think of the rejection.

Carmen observed that the three of them were going to have a typical "Hi-Guy" conversation and drifted over to Felice to keep her company – while awaiting Lynn Adler's arrival. "Understand you're in publishing," she opened amiably.

"Yes," Felice answered, watching the brawny bartender place her daiquiri on the bar, along with a scotch and water for Carmen. "The dull part, though." Felice laughed.

"What could be dull in such a fascinating business?" Carmen inquired. "All those authors and fancy parties," she added, though she'd already surmised Felice Capezio wouldn't be on the guest list.

Felice shrugged. "That's for the bigshots. I'm in permissions."

"What's that?" Carmen inquired, reaching for their drinks and handing Felice's to her.

"What it sounds like. Somebody wants to quote a passage from one of our titles, and I have to decide whether or not to give permission, should we charge a fee, or whatever."

"Really all that dull?"

She smiled and nodded. "But secure, like civil service."

THE CRUISE

At that moment, Erika and Charlene entered the lounge, and Carmen went over to introduce herself, then the others to them. She was dead certain she'd met Erika Schultz before, but couldn't place where or when. The gay world was an insular one, and anyone who moved about in urbane lesbian circles was bound to meet everyone at one point or another.

But there was a vibrancy about Erika that no one would ever be likely to forget totally. Tall, graying hair worn loosely flowing, wide and candid gray eyes filled with mirth, and a smile that would charm a snake out of its hole. Yes, Carmen had definitely met her somewhere, but she said nothing.

She took in the agent with skillful nonchalance. While Erika was, no argument, somewhat tomboyish, Charlene was a pork sausage of TNT. She was as rigid as a Prussian officer at inspection: taut, mean, and definitely hostile; C-List trying to cut it with the A-List. Her faded blonde hair was worn in the style of the late forties – very Ella Raines, or Alexis Smith trapped in the wrong beauty parlor. Her jewelry was definitely Cartier and her accessories were Gucci, but it was impossible to nail down her clothes other than that they were expensive. *She needn't bother*, Carmen thought ruefully; *whatever she wears will look like a gunnysack on that body!*

"Bernie! You ol' sonuvagun, where the hell have you been?" Erika burst out, striding toward the bar with a grin of happy recognition.

"Erika Schultz! You shithead you! I'll be damned!" Bernie exclaimed, matching Erika's happy surprise. "Been workin' around Detroit last few years. Carmen here got me this job. You remember Carmen, don'tcha?"

Erika turned slowly, trying to remember the woman's face. "Hell, you know I'm rotten at such things – "

"Carmen," Bernie called out. "Remember when I was working that gay bar down in the Village? It was ol'

Erika here what owned it, remember?"

Of course! Carmen thought, suddenly recalling all too well the huge crush she'd had on the owner of that bar. Smooth, all smiles, with a glowing good looks seldom seen on people who live in bars. She'd been entirely too green and young for Erika to notice her then, but Carmen had not forgotten Erika's easy sophistication. "You're joking!" she said, shaking her head with a disbelieving smile. "I thought you looked familiar, but I wasn't quite sure."

Erika extended her hand and clasped Carmen's with a warm grip. "Hell, that was twenty years ago! How'd I ever let you into my place back then? You'd have gotten me busted for sure! What were you? Sixteen?"

Charlene had been vainly trying to get Bernie's attention so she could order a drink, her mouth a sliver of tight resentment as the three women talked. "Miss . . .?" she said to Bernie.

"Ain't this somethin' though?" Bernie said directly at Charlene, but oblivious to the short woman's needs.

"We've got a lot of catching up to do!" Erika said.

"Sir . . . ?" Charlene tried again, sarcastically.

"W-what? Oh, sorry, little lady. What'll it be?"

Charlene perched her ample buttocks on the small barstool, an evil glint of success in her eyes. "Martini, Tanqueray, straight up, twist of lemon, and a dash of salt."

"Salt?"

"Yeah, she's a salt freak. Don't let it bother you," Erika said, interrupting her animated conversation with Carmen, and trying to include Felice so she wouldn't feel left out.

"It's your gut, lady," Bernie said, back to her professional manner, then her eyes opened wide mid-sentence.

Carmen didn't have to turn around to know that Lynn Adler had just entered the lounge. Even without Bernie's agape stare, Carmen could feel Lynn's presence.

Too, Lynn was wearing Givenchy perfume. Though Carmen never wore it herself, it was a scent that drove her wild no matter who was wearing it; but on Lynn Adler, she wasn't sure she'd be able to control herself. Mustering every gram of calm assurance she'd learned over the years, Carmen turned slowly and walked over to the young woman. "How nice you could join us, Ms. Adler," she offered, then impulsively put her arm through Lynn's and led her to the circle at the bar. Lynn's arm seemed cool to her touch, young and smooth, excitingly pale compared to Carmen's deep tan. And she was excruciatingly careful not to let her arm touch Lynn's breast. *No cheap tricks with this cookie*, she thought.

All conversation stopped as if on cue while each of the women took in Lynn's feline and graceful movements. Introductions were made, but only Felice and Erika seemed unaffected beyond the first surprise of seeing so lovely a creature in their midst.

Lynn smiled at each, enigmatically, and swiftly filed their faces and names in her mind. It was too soon to tell for sure, but she doubted that any of them would qualify as one of her lovers. At least, not that night – though Erika showed promise.

¤ ¤ ¤

"Christ!" Charlene fumed. "You can take the woman out of the bar, but you sure can't take the bar out of the woman!"

Erika stretched out on her bunk, hands beneath her head, and her long legs crossed at the ankles. "What's wrong with saying hello to old friends?" She was pleased with herself, feeling almost the way she used to; at the top, fun-loving, able to pluck any woman of her choosing. Wow! But it'd been a long time since she'd felt this good.

THE CRUISE

"Listen, you cheap barkeep! You're a writer now, not a tavern owner for the world's weirdos!"

"You're shrieking, Charlene – you know that always turns your face red. So I'm a writer now – does that mean I have to lie about my past?"

"*Yes!*" she hurled vehemently. "Forget your fuckin' past! Try to act like a lady, like someone of note and breeding!"

Erika rolled her gray eyes upward, but her spirits were entirely too high for the woman to really get to her. "Well, I'm not, Charlene. I come from a dirt-poor mining town, and I've made more fortunes than you could dream of."

"And you've lost every one of them," Charlene hissed.

"So? That didn't stop you from trying to catch me for the whole time. You were always hanging around in my bars, all moon-eyed and adoring. The only thing that's changed, really, is that you've finally got me."

Charlene's shoulders sagged, and she sat down on the edge of her bunk, tears welling in her hazel eyes. "Why do we always have to fight?" she asked softly, her attitude totally altered.

Erika rolled over, facing Charlene, and for a moment, she truly felt sorry for her. The woman was a paradox, a walking contradiction. "There's an old proverb, Charlene – goes something like 'Beware of what you ask for . . . you might get it.' I think that's what's happened to you. You wanted me for all those years, and when you finally got me, I wasn't what you'd expected."

The woman looked at her for a few seconds, blinking rapidly and nervously playing with a button on her blouse. "You were so glamorous to me, so terribly popular and unattainable. Look at you now. . . ." Charlene's voice trailed off.

Erika chuckled. "I'm the same person, Charlene, except that I'm on my uppers. But I'll get back to the top again, don't you worry."

"Erika?"

"Hmm?"

"Do you want to . . . have sex?"

"No."

"Why not?" she asked in a small voice.

"Because," Erika said, almost embarrassed for her, "you don't enjoy it. What for?"

"I can't help it that I'm frigid . . . I could make love to you?"

Erika stood up and crossed over to the bathroom, then stood straight. Without even looking at Charlene, she asked: "What is the sound of one hand clapping?"

¤ ¤ ¤

"Jeez, did you ever see anything like that dame?" Donna asked, pulling off her Western boots and sweatsocks, rubbing the ball of her foot against her other leg. "I could hardly eat my supper!"

Sandy sat down next to her, putting both her arms around Donna's neck. "You're not really all that attracted to her, are you, hon?" She nuzzled closer to Donna.

She grinned and playfully pulled Sandy down on the bed, kissing her lightly on the lips. "Hell, doll, about as much as I'd be attracted to Sophia Loren! I mean, baby, I can appreciate real beauty when I see it – but I know when I'm outclassed!"

"I know what you mean," Sandy said. "When she first came into the lounge, I thought maybe I should curtsy or something."

Donna laughed. "She sure is something else, all right."

Sandy twisted in Donna's arms, pushing her small

breasts against Donna's chest. "Do it to me?" she asked quietly.

"Hell, again?" Donna inquired, still smiling.

"I want to be sure you're mine, that you're not thinking of straying with that model. . . ."

"No way, doll, no way," Donna answered. Yet for an instant, as she brought her mouth to Sandy's, she thought about Lynn Adler.

¤ ¤ ¤

The night air was crisp as Felice strolled leisurely toward the prow of the ship. She hugged her sweater about her lean body as the chilly wind caught her clothes and played through her short hair. "Brr," she said to herself, looking forward to the next morning when she could get out in the sun and start working on a tan.

The night was clear and the stars glimmered like city lights when seen from fifteen thousand feet aloft. *It was upside down,* Felice thought. *I should be thinking in terms of gems sparkling, or twinkling diamonds. Only I could come up with a picture that's upside down!* She smiled and leaned over the ship's railing just before the bulwark. Lights from below deck illumined the churning and foaming water, soft white sprays against grayish-greens as the bow slashed the ocean's surface and swooshed the inky water aside. There was something very sad about it; no, not sad – isolating. She felt all alone.

I'm crazy. That's what it is, she told herself silently. *Here I am, more than three thousand miles from home, on board a resurrected* Titanic, *with three hundred – count 'em – bona fide lesbians, and* I *feel all alone!*

Strains of live music reached her as the wind gently shifted, and Felice considered the idea of going down to the third deck to the Fish Net Disco. Aptly named, she was sure, and she recalled seeing the poster in the lounge, with the color photograph of Kellie O'Reilly and her All-Girl Band. She didn't think she was quite up for that yet. Maybe tomorrow night.

"It's beautiful, isn't it," a voice said behind her, not in questioning but as a statement.

Felice turned her face over her shoulder and saw an attractive woman of about forty-five. She had totally white hair, worn in a French twist, and the bluest eyes Felice had ever seen. "Yes," she answered, not knowing what else to say.

" 'Illimitable ocean without bound, without dimension,' and something, something, something. Then, 'And time and place are lost.' Do you remember what comes in the middle?"

Felice smiled. "No."

"It's from *Paradise Lost*, but I'm afraid too many years have passed for me to still recall it all."

"Perhaps there's a library aboard. Maybe you could look it up." Now that she was closer, Felice could see that the woman was older; still exceptionally attractive, but at least in her mid-fifties.

"I doubt that they'd bother with a library," the woman said, laughing. "I don't think reading is part of the organized activities, do you?"

"No, you're probably right." Felice smiled.

"What's your impression? I mean, about the cruise and our fellow – or should I say 'sister'? – passengers?"

Felice turned around then, leaning her elbows on the wooden rail, and pulled the corners of her mouth down. "It's a little too soon to tell. Food's good. Accommodations are comfortable, if not luxurious."

"But the . . . women?"

"A curious mixture, I suppose. Better than what I'd thought they might be like. And I like the idea of a single-class cruise, no segregation because of finances or color."

The woman nodded affably. "I'd guess it's about seventy-thirty, butch to fem, wouldn't you? But I agree with you, I too had worried that I'd be the only feminine woman aboard." She played with a thick wedding ring on her left hand, twisting it around absently. "Did you see that table with the militant crowd?"

Felice shook her head. "No, what seating was it?"

"First. I felt as if I were witnessing a bundt rally."

"I'll keep an eye out," she said. "This is my vacation, and I've no interest in fire-and-brimstone proselytism."

Two couples came giggling top deck just then; young, full of energy and out for a good time. They all waved in acknowledgement of Felice's and the older woman's presence, then disappeared down the promenade, thumping loudly against the suspended lifeboats.

"Kids," the woman said. "Just kids... except they're gay as geese. My name's Margaret, by the way. And you're . . .?"

"Felice." Sensing that the woman was holding back something, wanting to confide but uncertain, she decided it would be best to take her leave. Her own mood wasn't so elevated that she could afford to risk someone else's bummer. "Well," Felice said slowly and stretching, "guess I'll tuck myself in for the night."

"You're alone on this cruise?" the woman asked with a slight tightness in her voice.

"Yes, quite."

"W-will I see you tomorrow?"

Felice felt terribly uncomfortable, not knowing how to handle the tension she felt in this person. What had started out as a friendly enough encounter had suddenly become much more, but undefinably so. She didn't know for sure what it was. Quiet desperation? A silent pleading to be held and reassured? Felice didn't know. "I'll be at the pool all morning," she said softly.

The woman smiled, nodded, but said nothing.

"Good night," Felice added, then crossed the deck to the starboard side and headed for the stairs toward her cabin. The tat-tatting of a snare drum reached her ears, along with the strained sounds of brass bleating out "The Stripper" from *Gypsy*. She had no difficulty imagining what the Fish Net Disco dancers were doing right then. No difficulty at all.

CHAPTER THREE

ERIKA SCHULTZ SAT at her portable typewriter, watching the sea's horizon rhythmically coming into view as the ship rolled slightly. There had been countless times when she'd tried to figure out just when it was she'd permitted herself to be talked into this writing crap. If anyone knew nothing about how to be a writer, she was it. Damn that Charlene to hell anyhow! Her first book had been something of a lark; see if she could do it, and all that. Hard work, to be sure, yet there has been a great deal of satisfaction in knowing that she, a high school graduate who'd spent her life fronting or owning gay bars, could possibly write a book worth publishing. Yet, she had. Hardcover, too, not a quickie paperback. *The* definitive pasta recipe book! Erika was a pasta freak; though her figure would never betray it. Two hundred and twenty-four pages on how to prepare pasta, its history, anecdotes, and even how to make your own; ten-ninety-five plus tax, retail.

The *Sacramento Bee* had given it a nice writeup; so had the *Chattanooga Times. The New York Times* had only given it a mention, in a special issue of the Book Review Section devoted to current cookbook releases. But that's all. Death would've been preferable. It was as if the book had never been published – and to all intents and purposes, it might just as well not have been. Except, there was that warm reward whenever Erika took the book down from its shelf and saw her name right on the dust jacket, repeated on the cover itself, on the spine, on the title page, the copyright page – it was like a reaffirmation of her existence, that she had a right to live, just like anybody else.

Maybe Charlene is right after all, Erika thought. *I'm not the way I used to be. Where's the fun? The laughter that came so easily? She's got me in over my fuckin' head, that's where it's at! I enjoyed researching the pasta book, and who the hell gives a shit about brilliant writing in a cookbook! But these cult religions, the runaways, the tragedy of punk kids who don't know what they're letting themselves in for – I'm just not qualified to write about that! No way!*

She stared at the blank piece of paper in the typewriter as if it were a deadly enemy. Then, carefully, almost childlike, she typed: F-U-C-K!

Erika rose from the makeshift desk, ran a well-shaped hand through her thick, shiny hair, and left the stateroom letting the door slam behind her. Charlene would be back from the ship's beauty parlor any moment, expecting to see her grinding out the end of the book, but Erika didn't give a damn. Let the old bag throw herself overboard!

She sauntered into the Neptune Lounge and sat down

at the bar, surprised to see Bernie on duty. "Hi, ol' buddy. How come you're working the morning shift?"

Bernie shrugged. "The baby butch who's supposed to be workin' got her monthlies – disgustin', ain't it?"

"Yeah, reckon so," Erika answered, amused.

"Bourbon an' water, same as always?"

She shook her head. "Nah. I quit the hard stuff a long time ago. Cigarettes, too."

"That's too bad."

Erika laughed good-naturedly. Of course, Bernie would look upon it as hard luck or deprivation! "Got any cheap white wine?"

"The cheapest!" Bernie leaned down and brought up an unlabeled half gallon of white wine. She poured a glass of it, her biceps flexing with the action. "How's it going, Rick?"

She smiled at the old nickname. "Nobody calls me that anymore, y'know it? Kinda miss it, though."

Bernie returned to putting out the setups before the luncheon crowd began. "It was a gas! There you were, lookin' for all the world like Ingrid Berman, right when *Casablanca* was showin' everywhere, with Bogie playing the part of Rick. It sure was a gas all right."

Erika took a sip of the wine, squinted bravely as it went down, then cocked her head as if surprised she'd survived. "That was sure one helluva long time ago. Which place did I have back then? The Melody Room?"

"No, you'd dumped that place already. Kickbacks to the fuzz was breakin' you. You'd opened up Truck Stop, over on Seventh Avenue, remember? Nice place. Good crowd. Tippers, too."

"Yeah, that's right."

Neither of them said anything for a few moments, but it was a comfortable silence. There were thousands of shared memories between the two; anything that could ever happen in a bar had happened to them both. The drunk commode-hugging dykes, the duck-tailed butches fighting over a floppy-hatted fem, the straight slummers looking down their noses and laughing at how Those People lived, the payoffs, the Syndicate muscling in . . . all of it. It was a world within a world, not especially different, but more intense. Jokes had to be funnier, tears more bitter, a buzz turned into a drunk. There was always an element of danger, of course; the police routinely raided gay joints, as much for the fun of it as for the pressure to buy them off. If you paid them enough, you could even let the women dance together to the jukebox. If you didn't pay, only one customer could go into the ladies room at a time – just in case. It had been a crazy period; manic in its microcosmic defiance of the illegality of homosexuality or lesbiansim.

And Erika had loved every damn moment of it! The liquor salesmen; Mafia-controlled jukebox concessions; the stench of stale liquor at four in the morning as they closed up for the night; the stragglers wanting just one more "for the road" even though they weren't driving–and always, without fail, that corner booth where Erika knew her current flame was impatiently waiting for her to clean out the till so they could climb into the sack together. She'd not lived with very many women; it wasn't really her style. She liked her freedom, and she had always been a fool for any pretty face that came along.

Those were the good old days, when all her clothes were tailor-made and her jewelry was designed especially for her. Italian shoes, English wool suits – the best, always the very best, made just for her. No two alike. She threw lavish private parties, rented yachts for weekends at the Hamptons, and was only seen with the most beautiful women in New York City. She didn't care how old they were – as long as they were stunning. Men were nice guys, pals; and occasionally, even fun to go to bed with – just to keep in practice. But women! Women were mysterious, smoldering, anxious to be loved by the most notorious lesbian in all the state. How often had Erika seen her mere touch bring shudders of delight?

". . . Doin' these days?"

Bernie's voice brought her back to the present. "Sorry, what'd you say?"

"Asked what you're up to nowadays. You got a club or what?"

"No," Erika answered slowly. "Not any more. I'm a writer now."

Bernie tucked in her chin, looking quizzically at her. "You've quit booze and fags, you're not in the bar business anymore . . . what the hell's wrong with you, Rick?"

She laughed. "Guess I'm getting old."

"What kind of stuff're you writin'? Didn't know you could."

"Oh, crap. Just crap." She gestured to have her wine glass refilled.

"Been published yet?"

"Oh yeah, sure. One book. Working on another now."

"What's it about?"

"Religious nuts."

"Bullshit you say! You don't know nothin' about that!"

"Right."

Bernie placed her palms squarely on the bar, and leveled her gaze at Erika. "Why don't you write about somethin' you know? Jesus, Rick! Do a book about all those years of running gay bars, about the kooks and the good times and the bad. You're crazy if you don't."

"Y'know, Bernie, you damn well might have something there."

The bartender lowered her eyes. "I've always known what's best for you, Rick. I've always cared –"

"I know, Bernie, I know." She fumbled in her pants

pocket, pulled out a five, and left it on the bar. Erika gave Bernie a two-finger salute from the forehead, ambled out of the lounge and began walking aimlessly. She couldn't afford to part with that fiver – but she also couldn't afford to listen to Bernie rehash her twenty years of loyal devotion. She'd have to think of a pretty good excuse to Charlene for spending that five bucks. *Damn that woman*, she thought, mindless of other passengers on deck. *The only thing she doesn't make me account for is toilet paper!*

But that's what happens, ol' girl, she reminded herself, *when you let someone else take over your life; it's your own damned fault.*

There was no real animosity in Erika's attitude toward Charlene. She bitched to herself a great deal about the woman's nagging dominance, but Erika was entirely too honest not to accept that she'd brought it on herself. When they'd gotten together she'd been farther down than she'd ever been in her entire life, and giving fifty a hard shove. Erika had been into a record-breaking depression. There was nothing left. The game was over. Any idiot with the capital could own a gay bar by then, and the Mafia no longer needed anyone to front the joints. Unless you allowed a traffic in drugs on the premises, even the police left you alone. For the past five years, running a gay bar in New York was as respectable as having a bakery. Maybe even more so. It seemed like everybody wanted to get in the act. Where it used to be that straights said "Some of my best friends are queer," now they were all dabbling in homosexuality, taking pride in their bisexuality and liberation from the restraints of monosexuality. It was chic to play both sides of the coin. But it left Erika with nowhere to go, nothing to do with herself.

She'd lost the last bar slowly, almost before she could see what was happening. The tenements were torn down one by one, luxury high-rises replacing them, and the clientele had drifted off gradually. Erika's specialty lay in her ability to keep the spirit of the fifties alive; a saloon-like atmosphere, catering to people from all walks of life, with a delicious illicit aura. The bulk of her customers were, to be sure, in their late forties or more; they liked the old songs on the jukebox, the ambience of their youth. Though kids came in with some frequency, they were seldom regulars, and they were all the same. Swaggering, overconfident, looking to see how the Old Folks managed to have a good time despite their Geritol and wheelchairs. And occasionally, the scared kids, looking to be brought out by someone older, experienced. Those were the ones Erika felt sorry for. Yet, she knew, leading a gay life would be far different for them from what it ever had been for her generation. Maybe not as exciting, but certainly safer and easier.

But she'd lost the place. In the old days, she'd been able to climb back to the top by taking on a job as the manager for the Syndicate, letting them put her name down on the liquor license – if anyone was going to get arrested, it would be she. After awhile, copping a little here and saving a bit there, she could buy a place of her own again and make out like a bandit. Her biggest problem had been that she'd never learned to save or invest money when she was riding on top. At those times, her ebullience and generosity knew no bounds; the flow of big money would never cease. Only when she was tapped out did she become thrifty, with her sole motive squarely set to get back on top.

It was then, six years ago, wondering what the hell to do with herself, that she'd run into Charlene at a party. *It's funny,* Erika reflected, *how you don't know who your real friends are till you're wiped out.* Most people avoided her like a leper, as if her bad luck would rub off on them; but some few, the real people, couldn't care less – they only wanted her to be healthy and happy. Those were the people who counted. Damn few of that kind around anymore.

Meeting Charlene again had been like a shot of adrenaline. She'd been thin, perplexed, and had a kind of stalked animal quality to her. Though Charlene couldn't have been described as genuinely attractive, much less having a good figure, still there'd been something elusively winning about her – sort of frightened, as if she needed a protector. Erika had seen the woman at her bars for years and years, popping up here and there, with this one or that one, but she'd never been Erika's type.

By then, feeling adrift and useless, Charlene's obvious infatuation was flattering and welcome. Charlene had pressed her phone number on her, damn near pleading Erika to call, and had never taken her eyes off Erika for the entire evening. When they finally did get together, Charlene fawned over her shamelessly; yet it was just what Erika needed at that point in her life. Somehow, someway, Charlene had managed to convince Erika that she should move in with her; that she'd "take care" of her. It was not the sort of thing Erika would ever have considered had she been at the top; but she'd been at the very bottom and nearly fifty years old, and for the first time in her life, feeling just a little scared. She'd moved in. And that was her first mistake.

Six years, Erika thought, *is one helluva long time!*

She spotted an empty deckchair, somewhat removed from the scores of others, and settled onto it, stretching her long limbs and turning her face into the sun. Faraway guffaws and giggles reached her from shuffleboard games, volleyball courts, and the swimming pool. Erika smiled to herself as she thought of all those women having a good time, comfortable in the realization that they didn't have to hide their emotions or relationships. Free. That's nice, she thought warmly, and was happy for them – for as long as it lasted.

"Miss Schultz . . .?"

Erika opened one eye slowly, only mildly disturbed by the interruption of her reverie. What she saw turned her stomach to jelly. Long, lovely legs; hips exposed by a hairline bikini; a waistline that cried for an embrace; firm, high breasts that promised swift response; and a chiseled face with the expression of a blonde madonna.

She opened the other eye, grinning in recognition.

"I-I'm Lynn Adler. We met . . . last night . . . if you recall?"

She had a body that was created for caressing. "I've a good memory, Ms. Adler. I may be getting old, but the mind is still alert," she said, laughing lightly.

"Old!" Lynn scoffed, then seated herself sideways next to Erika's ankles. "Distinguished, yes. Mature, certainly. But not *old*!"

Erika rested her head against the canvas and speculated what Lynn Adler was up to. *Why is this beautiful chicken coming after the turkey?* she wondered, with the almost forgotten feeling of the chase coming back to her full force. The way Lynn was facing, with the sun dancing off her body, every contour was delicately highlighted; the barest hint of pelvic bone before the gentle indentation preceding the soft outline of the abdomen. Her breasts rose and fell with each breath, oblivious to what memories they stirred within Erika; the wrenching joy of placing her face against such softness, fondling, sucking. . . . It had been a very, very long time since Erika had responded to a woman's body – just looking at it – so strongly. But then, Lynn was terribly young, and exceptionally attractive. Something wasn't right, though, and Erika knew it. Stunning young women simply didn't go on the make for over-the-hill lesbians; especially not down-and-out ones . . . not that Lynn would know about that.

After a moment, Lynn broke the silence. "You're a writer, aren't you? Or was it the other woman?"

Erika gazed into the girl's fern-green eyes trying to figure out what she wanted. "Yes, I'm the writing half of our vaudeville show."

Lynn averted her eyes, leaned down and adjusted the strap of her sandal. Erika didn't fail to notice the way the movement had revealed the crevice between her buttocks, or the way her breasts plumped as they pressed against her thighs.

"I, well, I do a little writing myself," Lynn said shyly. "Probably just amateur level, but I find it very rewarding. I've often thought, though, that I might like to become a serious writer. You know, make a living at it, and all that. I don't suppose I have the brains for it. . . ."

Erika had heard this approach, or its many variations, dozens of times. It didn't matter where she went, everyone in the world thought she could be a writer – if only she tried, or had a little "advice." This time, however, Erika's curiosity had been piqued. "It doesn't take all that much intelligence, Ms. Adler –"

"Please call me Lynn."

Erika smiled. "What's your nickname?"

"Why, I don't have one," Lynn said, matching Erika's smile.

"Then I'll call you Legs – as long as my old lady isn't around. Okay?"

Lynn nodded, an expression of ingenuous conspiracy on her face. "Do you find my legs attractive?"

"I'd have to be blind not to!"

The color of Lynn's eyes changed to a darker green, as if her thoughts were casting a shadow over them. "And what shall I call you . . . when your old lady isn't around?"

"Rick. Call me Rick," Erika said, a tingle of anticipation running through her.

Lynn twisted slightly on the chair, placing her hand on the other side of Erika's legs and jutting her breasts forward. "You've the most wonderful smile I've ever seen on anyone . . . Rick."

"Thank you," Erika said, her eyes dropping to the

youthful mounds beneath the bikini top. There was no doubt in Erika's mind that this delectable creature wanted to go to bed with her – who gave a damn why!

"Would it be asking too much if I showed you some of my writing? I mean, just a couple of pages or so. Maybe you could tell me whether or not I've any ability . . .?"

"Oh, I'm sure you've got ability, Legs," Erika teased gently, acutely aware that her long-dormant clitoris was reacting to the sight of this beauty who so plainly wanted to have sex with her. It had been ages since anyone had turned her on like that; she'd almost come to believe that she was definitely out of the sex game, dead inside, as dried up as a burnt-out furnace. Her renewed awakening was exhilarating, challenging. Erika didn't feel "young again," but she felt alive once more; sure of herself, cognizant of her own expertise at lovemaking. Desire and conquest.

"Well, well, I thought I might find you out here," Charlene's voice chopped through. "Have you managed to finish the book so soon?" Charlene asked with a sweet-and-sour voice, "or are you researching a new one before you've finished the old?"

She was standing with the sun behind her so that all Erika could really see was a tall lump – or a short mountain. It didn't surprise her that Charlene had come stalking after her; it was the sort of thing she'd come to expect from her. "Neither, Charlene, I'm resting."

"From *what*!"

"Charlene's not just a literary agent, Lynn, but she happens to be *my* agent as well. That gets tricky sometimes. Hard to goof off," she added calmly.

"You've been goofing off for fifty-six years. Now, I think it's time you faced your age, and your obligations, and got back to work."

Neat, Charlene, very neat. You've told the girl just how old I am, that I'm a shirker, and who's boss. Sighing in genial resignation, Erika swung her legs to the deck and stood up. "You'll never learn how to have fun at this rate," she said, looking down at Charlene.

"Fun is for after," the woman said, "not before."

"No, Charlene – fun is for during, but you don't understand that. S'long, Lynn, see you around."

Silent though Lynn had been during the brief exchange, Erika didn't miss the look on the young woman's face, a bemused expression that indicated she viewed the interruption as something that only heightened appetite.

¤ ¤ ¤

Donna sat at the round table nearest to the porthole, studying her cards carefully, and furtively taking in how many chips she had left before her. She'd already lost close to thirty dollars, however she knew it only meant the others would think she was on a losing streak. That was only to the good. Now that she'd drawn a king-high full-house, they would be bound to think she was bluffing. She tugged at her chin as if the mortgage depended on what she did next.

"C'mon, c'mon," Barbara coaxed. "You gonna meet my raise or aint'cha?"

"Give me a second, darn it," Donna said, pulling a Camel out from the pack, lighting it with her Zippo with the Los Angeles County emblem on it. "Tell you what," she said, trying to make her lopsided grin look like a forced smile. "I'll not only meet you, but I'm going to raise you twenty!"

"Aw, come on, guy! You're crazy!" Mac said, a hefty woman of about thirty-five, with a man's haircut, and wearing a tee-shirt that read: "Wimmin Do It Better." It was easy to read since Mac wasn't wearing a bra and her pendulous breasts hung well beneath the slogan.

"You're just making it rough on the rest of us, guy," Pinky mumbled unhappily. She too had been losing rather heavily over the past two hours.

"Get you a beer, hon?" Sandy said, coming up behind Donna and resting her elbow on Donna's shoulder.

"Yeah, sure. Thanks, doll," Donna said, paying no attention actually. "Now look," she reasoned, "there's no way I'm going to get back what I've lost so far if you all chicken out. I've got a hot hand finally, and I'm raising with another twenty. Match it or fold."

"That lets me out!" Pinky said, throwing her cards facedown on the table. "I don't think you've even got a pair Donna, but I ain't gonna throw away my money to find out."

Donna kept her face a careful blank. "Up to you, then, Mac. You in this game, or out?"

The overweight woman cupped her fingers and ran her nails slowly over her cheek, as if assessing the growth of her beard. Then she rocked in her chair, a slow smile coming to her face. "I think Pinky's right, Big Don – I think you've got nothing but crap in your hand, an' I'm willing to bet on it. I'll meet Barbara's raise of five, your twenty, and I'm gonna sweeten the pot by raisin' you both with another ten!"

"Sweetie? Don't forget we've gotta pay for this trip on the MasterCard when we get home . . . don't go spending it all before, y'hear?"

Mac winked at Barbara and Donna. "I won't, darlin', I promise," she called to the obese woman who sat with the other wives of the players. "Okay, guys, what'dya say?"

"Shee-it!" Barbara said, puffing on the half-smoked cigarette dangling from her lips. "Fucked if I do, an' fucked if I don't."

"Now who's stalling?" Donna asked, smirking.

"Fuck off," Barbara said absently, concentrating on

her hand. "All right, all right. I'll stay in, but I'll cut your balls off if you ain't gonna make it worthwhile!" Her short, nail-bitten fingers shoved thirty dollars' worth of chips into the pot.

"Here's my ten," Donna said. "Let's see what you've got, Mac. It better be good!"

The woman glanced cockily from Barbara to Donna, her thin mouth twisting up at one corner, then fanned the five cards out before her. "Eat your hearts out, guys – ace-high straight!"

"Shee-it!" Barbara moaned, tossing her cards down like hot coals.

Mac began to gather the chips toward her, laughing deep in her throat.

"Whoa!" Donna said, placing her hand on Mac's. "Hang on a second, ol' chum."

The woman hesitated, frowning.

"Put your baby blues on these!" Donna peeled off her hand card by card. She was showing off and she knew it. For some reason, whenever she was around people like Mac and Pinky, Donna tended to strut a little. She meant no harm by it; it was just a reaction.

"Well, I'll be damned!" Barbara said, her eyes wide.

Mac cocked her head and relinquished the pot. "Right on, Big Don. You sure had me fooled!"

"All right, you guys, that's enough now!" one of the waiting women called from the couch against the wall of the fourth-deck playroom. "You been playing cards for hours now."

"Yeah, that's right," another said churlishly.

They looked at each other appreciatively. "I'll let you try to win it back later," Donna said, rising and stretching. "How about a beer on me?"

"Least you can do!" Mac said, pounding a fist against Donna's shoulder.

Donna feinted with a left, laughing, and the four of

them crossed over to the small bar that had been set up in the gameroom. A wiry woman about five-foot-five pulled out one Coors, two Buds, and a Michelob, shoving them toward the women as they approached. "Sure ain't gonna get rich on you guys, never drinkin' nothing but beer," she said amiably.

"Hell, you forget that we're *big* tippers!" Donna said, then led the way to the conversation-pit arrangement where the others were waiting.

"That's your second beer in less than fifteen minutes," Sandy said, as if it hurt her feelings.

"Don't worry, Sandy," Donna said, sinking onto the couch next to her and patting her leg. "I just won us a bundle, so don't start nagging at me."

"That just means that Mac's lost!" the mammoth woman said, her face a mean threat.

"Nah," Donna intervened. "Only that she didn't win this time. We have a lot of time to come out even!"

"Oh yeah, sure," Barbara concurred facetiously.

Donna leaned back, putting her booted feet on the table before them. Hell, this was the life! she thought. No mosquitoes, no cooking out, no worrying about hookups or water. Just laying around, relaxing with your own kind of people who didn't have a lot of la-di-da ways about them. She was mighty glad they'd decided on this cruise – especially about the one hundred and fifty she'd just won. If that kept up, she'd be able to trade in their camper on a Winnebago when they got back home again! If these turkeys didn't know how to play poker any better than that, she'd sure as hell have more than enough for a downpayment when they got back to L.A.

Only half listening to the easy conversation about her, feeling a little drowsy from the beers, Donna fleetingly thought about the dogs at the kennel, hoping they were all right. Bojangles and Mutt had always gone with them, wherever it might be, but there'd been no getting around the rules for this cruise: No Pets! Well, they'd get along all right; might even be good for them, teach them a little appreciation.

". . . So I told that smokie there was no way I could be pullin' that trailer up Interstate 5 at no double nickel!"

". . . What'd he say?"

". . . Said I was a goddam liar!"

". . . Shee-it! What'd you do?"

". . . Was gonna poke him in the face, that's what! But Carol here wouldn't let me."

". . . You'd punch out a smokie?"

". . . Why the hell not?"

Yes, it was a good life. They had their small house in the San Fernando Valley, near the freeway so she could get downtown easily – depending on traffic, of course, but her hours weren't the peak ones. They had the kids, and good friends to come by for cookouts or get drunk with on weekends; their jobs were secure and building tenure. Another twenty-three years, and she'd be able to retire; maybe move to the desert, if she could talk Sandy into retiring early. Sandy was only thirty-seven, but she was so naive that Donna often thought of her as just a little tyke. Showing a few lines now, getting a little thick around the middle, but that was okay. She was a good cook, kept the house clean, and never let herself forget that Donna's job came first. She was also a mighty good lay. What more could anyone want?

"How's it going?"

Donna straightened up, startled to hear Carmen Navasky's voice. *Won't I* ever *get over feeling like we've been caught?* she asked herself derisively. "Fine, Carmen, just fine," she managed to answer at length, feeling less guilty and sheepish.

The others answered similarly, yet Donna could sense their discomfort. This Navasky broad wasn't like them; she was strictly the Gold Earring Set, the ones who could pass anywhere and who didn't say "ain't." There was something intimidating about those people, like they couldn't face themselves and had to play a game all the time. It was sort of sad, she thought. Donna was sure they had one foot in each camp, unable to move forward or backward without endangering their status in one world or the other.

"Now, I really want to remind you," Carmen said, pushing her dark brown hair away from her eyes, "that this is a uni-class tour. You don't have to stay on this deck, or confine yourselves to any one section of the ship. Strictly democratic," Carmen finished, smiling brilliantly.

Bet her teeth are capped, Donna thought, fascinated by the perfect row of sparkling whiteness.

"Sure, sure," Mac answered for them all. "We just happened to get into a game, that's all. We'll be on up later, isn't that right, guys?"

Each nodded her assent or muttered an unenthusiastic "Yeah."

"Well, if you don't," Carmen said gaily, "the rest of us are going to swarm all over the place and you'll wish you had. See you later," she added, and left the gameroom with her fashionably high heels clicking sharply on the parquet floor.

The room was quiet for a few moments, then Sandy burst out laughing raucously. "If it's so democratic, how come we're down here, and they're up there?"

Donna grinned mirthfully, hugging Sandy to her. "Because they're the gold earring crowd, doll, and we're strictly the camper set."

"Shee-it! What's wrong with that?" Barbara asked.

"Nothing," Donna replied. "Just don't tell them, or they'd panic."

"Let's have another beer!" Mac said, and they all fell into their former ease with one another.

CHAPTER FOUR

BEYOND THE LOUNGE where Donna and the others were, at the ship's aft, was the swimming pool. Felice was at the far end, on the port side, sunning herself on a plastic deck chair. It was December 21 and she idly wondered what the weather was like back in Manhattan. Smiling to herself, she knew it was a senseless thing to be thinking; it could be snowing lightly or a blizzard, or an absolutely lovely day. Whatever it was, though, Felice was glad that she had decided to spend her extra week's vacation at home, tidying up all the things she preferred to ignore during the rest of the year: defrosting and cleaning the refrigerator; mending seams and sewing buttons back onto clothes that had sat in a corner for months; writing letters to out-of-state friends who had sent her birthday cards; along with the sundry other things that seemed to make up the duller side of her life.

And she thought about her friend Ann. She'd have a great deal to tell her when she got back; especially since the passengers aboard the S.S. *Sisterhood* were a far more heterogeneous group than Ann had predicted. But then, Ann always did look at the bleak side of things, though Felice had never understood why. Wasn't it far more positive to search out the good than to dwell on the bad? Oh well, that was the way Ann was, and Felice knew she'd have to go a long way to find a better friend.

Realizing that she had her arms folded across her midriff, blocking the sun, Felice moved her arms to her sides, feeling the penetrating rays on her body with lazy gratitude. The salty smell from the sea was conveyed by a light breeze as the ship moved forward, and the only sounds were the laughter of others around the pool, the throaty splash as someone dove in, and the steady, dull humming of the engine room somewhere in the belly of the ship.

The sea was calm that day, and the only motion was the gentle forward-aft nosing through the unbelievably blue Pacific. She had no idea of how many knots per hour they were doing, but Felice was confident they were in no rush. And that too made her feel good. Her eyes closed against the sun, she was deliciously comfortable. Someone not too far away lighted a cigarette and it smelled divine, tempting her to sit up and light one of her own – but it was too much trouble.

"Is this chair taken?"

Blocking the sun with a manicured, tapered hand, Felice opened her dark brown eyes to glance at the newcomer, then smiled graciously. "No, it's all yours," she said cordially.

About thirty or so, the woman was petite and feminine in a one-piece bathing suit, with a terrycloth robe over her shoulders and leather thongs on her feet. Dark red hair pulled back in a ponytail revealed a heart-shaped face, lightly freckled. Knees together,she lowered herself onto the chaise longue as if she'd learned how to do it at Bryn Mawr, then reached into the straw satchel she'd placed on the deck and pulled out a bottle of suntan lotion. "My name's Harmony Bourns," she declared as she rubbed the oily substance across her shoulders.

"Felice Capezio," she responded. "That's a very strange first name," she added, an expression of surprised amusement on her face.

Harmony shrugged as she worked the lotion down her arm. "My mother was an early hippie. At least, that's what she claims. My poor brother really got it socked to him, though."

"Oh? What's his name . . . Counterpoint?"

Harmony laughed briefly. "No, it's Chief Sitting Bull . . . after the Indian chief who defeated Custer. At least he can be called Chief, which is some consolation, I guess."

Felice's natural curiosity got the better of her and she sat up, digging into her linen jacket pocket for her cigarettes and lighter. "Do you mean to tell me that your mother *really* named him that? Why?"

"To be different, I guess. You know, flout convention and all that sort of thing. Mother says it was commonplace in the fifties."

Felice's oval face broke into an incredulous smile. "Poor guy! Chief Sitting Bull Bourns. Now, *that's* a head twist for you!" She watched as her new companion stretched out, liking what she saw. Small, pert breasts, skin like milk glass, an exceptionally small waist; her hips were perhaps just a bit too large, but Felice always thought women should have full hips – unlike her own, which were narrow.

"Mother talks a great deal about that period in her life," Harmony said. "We were both born out of wedlock;

she takes great pride in that."

Felice laughed. "She sounds like quite a character."

"Mother? Oh yes, she certainly is. And she gets more so all the time."

"Well, you seem to love her nonetheless."

"Oh, let's say that I'm fond of her. She can be tedious at times, but she means well. I think my father is the one who bears the brunt of her unconventional ways."

"Did they finally get married?"

Harmony turned onto her side to face Felice. "Oh, he's not our real father . . . he adopted us after marrying mother."

"What happened to your dad?" Felice could hardly believe her ears; the woman was revealing all these things with all the dramatic impact of a marketing list.

"He split. Didn't even talk about marriage, according to mother. Told her that parental responsibility was for Establishment cop-outs and he wanted no part of it."

"What was she supposed to do? Drown you?"

"I guess. But she didn't."

"Well, I'm certainly glad of *that*!"

"Me too."

For a moment, Felice wondered if Harmony was putting her on. "And what does your stepfather do?"

"Jim's a banker."

"A banker!"

Harmony smiled. "Uh-huh, and every bit as stuffy as most people think bankers are. I'll never understand what he saw in mother, much less why he married her. And they're always arguing," she concluded tonelessly.

Some of the women in the pool had begun tossing a huge plastic ball about, splashing water everywhere, squealing and giggling, and Felice's attention was taken away from Harmony for a second. For some reason, their activity surprised Felice; she would expect men to behave in that manner – showing off, rowdy – but not women. Obviously, her preconceived notions were incorrect. . . .

"Anyway," Harmony continued, "they've been married for twenty-eight years now, so I guess their marriage can't be all that bad."

"Maybe he likes living with danger," Felice quipped good-naturedly.

"He never knows when he comes home what he'll find," Harmony said. "Mother's as like to be stark naked, seated on the living room floor in the lotus position, as she is to be Mother Earth hausfrau, in jeans and apron, baking apple pie."

"Must make it tough on him to bring home unexpected dinner guests," Felice said.

"I guess. But I think he gets a vicarious kick out of her zaniness. Not that he'd admit it, of course."

"Oh, of course," she answered just as the frolicking ballplayers in the pool became just a little too rambunctious. "Hey," Felice called, swiping at the water they'd splashed on her legs.

"Sorry," one of them yelled back.

Felice's momentary ire subsided quickly; it was, after all, only water. "Do you . . . take after your mother?" she inquired hesitantly. There was something about Harmony that made Felice feel as if she were years and years older.

She shook her head, her ponytail swaying with the motion. "No, I'm a lesbian."

"Yes, I know, but I meant . . . in other ways?"

"No. I'm much more like Jim. The best schools, top student, queen of the prom . . . all that stuff."

"And what do you do now? For a living, I mean."

"I'm a pediatrician with a practice in Sacramento."

"A pediatrician!"

Harmony touched the whiteness of her thigh as if testing for how well cooked she might be, then draped her robe across her legs. "Why are you so surprised?"

"I don't know . . . I shouldn't be."

"Not anymore. Are you from a small town where women just don't have serious careers?"

"Me?" Felice laughed. "I live in New York City."

"Then you have no excuse, really," Harmony replied archly. "Know what my brother, Chief, does for a living?"

"How could I?"

"He's a telephone operator for Ma Bell. *He* takes after mother . . . can't hold a job and doesn't care."

Felice smiled, feeling foolishly outdated. "Maybe he figures he'll get married soon and it won't matter," she parodied.

"You really aren't very with it, are you," Harmony said with a small laugh. "Well, I guess I'd better go inside and get dressed for lunch. Nice talking to you, Felice."

She watched as Harmony gathered her things together and briskly walked away, her shoulders squared and her head high. Felice didn't believe for a moment that she had wanted to get ready for lunch – Harmony had been offended. At least, that's what she thought had driven Harmony away. It had been such an unusual encounter that Felice wasn't at all sure what she should make of it. *What a strange young woman,* she thought. *But then, with that mother of hers, what else could be expected?*

"Hi."

Jarred from her contemplation, Felice began to feel as if she were the ticket-taker at the Friendship Turnstile. "Oh, hi," she replied, recognizing Margaret.

"Can I buy you a drink?"

Dressed in a floral cotton print, with matching shoes and handbag, Felice was confident that Margaret had sought her out. But the idea of a drink had its appeal, and at least the woman wasn't a bit crinkly around the edges. "Sure, I'd love it," she responded, noticing that Margaret's white hair was perfectly in place, despite the breeze. Her French twist didn't have the glazed look of hairspray, so Felice had to assume that Margaret was just one of those enviable women who always looked perfect – no matter what.

"There's a bar in that lounge over there, but it's filled with stompers. We could go to the Acapulco Room, if you prefer."

"Oh, I don't really care."

"Well, I do," Margaret said somewhat shyly. "They make me terribly nervous with their loud talk and mannish imitations."

Felice said nothing to that remark, though she knew what Margaret meant. She had never been able to understand why any woman would want to find herself in heterosexual role-playing; wasn't the whole point of being a lesbian to be a woman who loves another woman? Why be a lesbian if you were going to live with someone who looked and acted like a man, who'd treat you exactly the same as a husband would? It had never made much sense to Felice. "Tell you what," she began. "I'm not really dressed properly for the upstairs lounge. Why don't we just have a drink over there, at the umbrella tables?"

"I don't think they have any service there," Margaret said nervously.

"Then I'll go into the lounge and get the drinks. How's that?"

"In there?" Margaret's blue eyes grew large with disbelief.

"Well, are they brandishing swords or something? I mean, it's safe, isn't it?" she asked, laughing.

Margaret's smile was sweetly appreciative. "You're a braver man than I am, Gunga Din," she remarked lightly, pulling a ladies' wallet from her handbag. "Bloody Mary, extra spicy."

"You're in charge of finding a table with an ashtray, and not too close to the ship's aquatic team in the pool," Felice said, accepting the billfold. "Back in a minute."

"What if you're not?" Margaret suddenly looked

worried, as if sending Felice into the lion's den while knowing full well she'd never be able to go into the lounge to save her if the beasts attacked.

Felice's brown eyes studied her for a second, wondering what she could be so worried about. "If I'm not, then you can figure I'm either a thief or I've converted to their ways."

"You wouldn't!" Margaret teased lightly.

"And I'm not a thief either," she said playfully, already heading across the deck to the lounge with the card and pool tables, the slot machines, and small bar. It was funny, she thought, how just minutes before she had felt like an alien to the planet, unable to relate to Harmony . . . and now she felt like a teenager, running off to do an errand for her mom. But at least Felice could communicate with Margaret; they were a generation apart, but they spoke the same language.

¤ ¤ ¤

Lynn Adler was seated at the round table that offered the best vantage point of any other in the Neptune Lounge, nursing a Diet Pepsi. Dressed in an emerald green halter top that really didn't cover very much – but showed off her eyes and cleavage – with white culottes, and thin-strapped high-heeled sandals, she looked as if she belonged in an advertisement for what chic young ladies were wearing on the QE II. Legs crossed at the knee, no one could miss the loveliness of her well-formed calf and trim ankle. But due to the sportiness of her attire, Lynn had decided to keep her jewelry understated; eighteen-karat stud earrings, and a twenty-four-inch gold rope necklace from Frances Klein's on Rodeo Drive in Beverly Hills – a graduation present from her parents. On her right hand, she wore a one-and-a-half-ounce solid gold ring in free form . . . a little gift from a woman married to a senator. Lynn couldn't remember her name anymore, not that she was very good with names in the first place. Unless, of course, someone could do something for her; in that case, she had a memory for names that would house a telephone directory.

Her ash-blonde hair was worn casually, with a chiffon scarf folded into a band to keep it off her face – thus showing off her exquisite facial planes.

Soft, piped in music played in the background, and from that spot in the lounge, Lynn could see everyone who entered or left; they would also see her. She thought about Erika Schultz and the way the older woman's eyes had devoured her earlier that day. *She is strikingly handsome,* Lynn decided. Older, lonely, and probably talented. These were good signs, and the only thing that bothered Lynn about Erika was that the woman was attractive. She would just have to wait. Maybe Erika would qualify ultimately, but it was a little too soon. She should not have sought Erika out that morning. It was a foolish move.

Glancing about the room, trying to avoid the garish pear-shaped chandeliers, Lynn assessed the patrons. Mostly couples, to her chagrin. Four Chicanas, freshly scrubbed and bursting with good health – and obviously friends – chatted and laughed among themselves. However, seated at the bar was a homely woman of about sixty or so. Her face was deeply lined, and she had looked Lynn up and down when she'd first come in, but had ignored her since.

Lynn's glance traveled past the backs of several others at the bar, then rested on a rather plain young woman, about Lynn's own age. No makeup, mouse-brown hair worn in a Prince Valiant cut, the woman was staring at Lynn. Just staring, her lips slightly apart, licking them frequently. When Lynn's eyes met hers, the woman smiled broadly, revealing far too much gum above her teeth. She lifted her beer to Lynn, and Lynn looked away instantly. Still . . . there was something. Uncertainty? Fear of rejection?

She risked another brief look – the woman was still staring at her, still licking her lips. *Horsey*, Lynn thought. *If she neighed, I wouldn't be surprised. Well, why not? Isn't this why I'm here?* Lynn raised one perfectly shaped eyebrow, then smiled insouciantly.

As if getting down from her saddle, the woman lumbered off the barstool and came toward Lynn, a silly grin on her long face. "Mind if I join you?"

Saying nothing, Lynn indicated the vacant chair with a nod of her head. *Jesus! She might as well have hay sticking out of her ears!*

"I'm Julia Fee," she said, seating herself clumsily.

"Phee? P-h-e-e?" Lynn gave Julia her most fascinated expression, as if Julia's name held the key to the universe.

"No, that's Scottish. Mine's f-e-e . . . we're Irish." She grinned again, never taking her eyes from Lynn's face.

"Isn't that interesting, though. I never knew that," Lynn said, looking over the rim of her glass as she sipped her Pepsi. "What do you do, Julia?"

"Me? Nothing. My dad's rich."

Lynn formed a pleasant smile designed to reveal detached amusement. "Oil, cattle, or politics?"

"Huh?"

"How did he acquire his wealth?" Lynn shifted gear and looked at Julia maternally. Wealthy or not, to do absolutely nothing was a waste of time, and Lynn didn't approve. However, she had to concede that in Julia's place, it probably wouldn't matter very much. She was so homely that age could only be a blessing . . . as it had been for Eleanor Roosevelt. All those teeth!

"Oh, uh, mostly oil."

"Doesn't he approve of you having a job, Julia? Don't

you get bored?"

"Oh, I do something. I travel a lot."

Lynn said nothing, knowing that most people could not bear silence following a statement and therefore felt compelled to say more.

"I'm from Pumpville, Texas . . . that's in Val Verde County, real near to the Mexican border." Her grin widened.

She suppressed a groan. Pumpville! She should have known! "Do you enjoy traveling? "

"Oh yeah, pretty much. My folks know I'm a lesbian, so they try to keep me away from home as much as they can."

"And just how did they find out?" Lynn asked, a slight frown of chagrinned concern creasing her forehead. "You didn't *tell* them!"

"Hell no," Julia replied, chuckling. "When I was in high school, I got a really big crush on one of my schoolmates, and one day, I just couldn't help myself. . . . I grabbed her in the ladies room and kissed her – right on the lips, too." She laughed louder.

"Really? But . . . ?"

"Oh, she was a sorehead about it. Pretended she wasn't a lesbian, too. Told her folks. Then all hell broke loose. In Pumpville, folks don't cotton to that sort of thing much."

"I imagine not."

"No they don't," Julia said as if Lynn had contradicted her. "So they packed me off to some damn Catholic school, thinking the nuns would put the fear of God in me."

"And did they?" Lynn's gaze shifted almost imperceptibly to see who was entering the lounge just at that moment. A couple. Uninteresting.

"Hell no," Julia guffawed. "I found out more about being a lesbian in a girls' school than I ever would've in Pumpville."

Lynn leaned back, resting her left arm over the chair, knowing full well that the position would reveal even more of her breasts. She pretended not to notice Julia's mesmerized gaze at the taut fabric over her nipple. The woman was a fool, she had no doubt of that. Every thought in her hick head was revealed as sharply as a finely tuned television picture. Only idiots permitted themselves to be all that transparent; yet, in a way, perhaps that was what appealed to Lynn. She smiled with a trace of a pout. "Then I suppose you're terribly experienced."

"Uh, well, not really. I tried to watch when I could, but mostly I just listened."

Lynn was disappointed. "Oh."

As if sensing that she had placed herself at a distinct disadvantage, Julia hastily said: "Well, I've had *some* experience since then!"

"I think you're bragging," Lynn replied with casual disdain, again shifting her glance toward the entrance to the lounge.

"Hey, lookie there," Julia said excitedly, as if espying a dinosaur over Lynn's shoulder.

Turning to see for herself, Lynn's brows rose quizzically. Behind the bar, two men were stacking cases of beer. "Men," she said softly, her voice trailing off.

"Big as life," Julia concurred. "Did you know there were any men on board? Other than the officers, I mean?"

Shaking her head, Lynn studied them clinically. Stocky, muscular, and young, they struck her as out of place as a man in a gynecologist's waiting room. "Do you suppose there are more?" She smiled as one of the men glanced her way.

"Beats me," Julia answered. "But I thought this was supposed to be all-lesbian. Even the ship's doctor is a woman – a black one, but she's a woman."

Lynn looked at Julia with amusement. "Does that bother you? That she's black, I mean?"

THE CRUISE

"Well, I'm not really prejudiced or anything, even though I'm from Texas. Hell, I never even *saw* a black person till I was about eleven or twelve, when my folks took me with them to San Antonio."

"But it does bother you," Lynn pressed lightly.

"A little," Julia admitted shyly. "How about you?"

Lynn gave a small shrug of dismissal. "I find black people exciting. Exotic, if you prefer."

Julia eyed her speculatively. "You ever been to bed with a black person?"

She hadn't expected the question to be posed in quite that way and Lynn hesitated briefly. "I almost did . . . once." Actually, she had, and it had been with a university student up in Santa Barbara – a young man. As a sophomore, she had felt daring and wicked despite the fact that interracial dating and marriages were quite ordinary by then. Still, from her affluent upbringing in Laguna, surrounded by her parents' influential friends and going to school with their children, Lynn had known that if her family ever found out there would be hell to pay. In that regard, her parents were of one mind: Welcome everyone to your home, but keep your distance except for people of your own class. Which, of course, translated to rich, important, Christian, and white.

And looking back on it, which Lynn had done a number of times, she realized later that she had probably come to love Elliot more than any other person she had ever met. He was tender, sensitive, intelligent – a far better student than she – and he never pretended to be anything other than what he was. When Elliot proposed to her, she had been deeply touched – but it was out of the question. Maybe her parents wouldn't have cut her out of the will, but they would have made her life a misery. Lynn had never been able to deal with confrontation; she hated ugly squabbles and name-calling . . . unless it was she doing the calling.

THE CRUISE

". . . I guess it's just because they look different."

"Hmm? What? I'm sorry," Lynn apologized, "I didn't quite hear you."

"Black people," Julia said. "Some of the Mez'cans, too. You know, not like us."

At the word "Mez'cans," one of the young women at the other table glanced their way like a cat sensing danger. But Lynn smiled at her – a reassuring, calming smile – and she turned her attention back to her friends. "I think, Julia, that if you intend to enjoy this cruise, you may want to choose your words a little more carefully."

"Huh? What for? I didn't mean any harm. . . . I'm just saying the truth of what's on my mind. Damn, but I'm tired of everybody being so thin-skinned, pretending everybody is equal."

Lynn's green eyes rested on Julia's face with marked patience. "Everyone *is* equal, Julia The difference is that not everyone has equal opportunity." Actually, Lynn cared little about such things. It was a grab-and-growl world; always had been and always would be. Academically, she felt a modicum of empathy; but in reality, inequities in life had nothing to do with her. However, Julia's superficiality had irked Lynn somewhat and it gave her a momentary sense of superiority to put Julia in her place. "Well, if you'll excuse me, I think I'll freshen up before lunch," she said sweetly, picking up her sunglasses from the table.

"Freshen up! Why, you look like a freshly minted silver dollar!"

Standing, Lynn looked down at Julia. "Thank you," she said demurely. "Perhaps we'll run into each other again."

Once back on the Promenade Deck, Lynn looked about to see if anyone "interesting" might be around. After that Julia Fee person, just about anyone would be an improvement. Good grief, if the passengers she'd seen on the cruise so far were any indication, she might just as well have stayed home and cruised the bars. However, that wasn't really true. Lynn didn't like going to gay bars; they were depressing. She far preferred to meet her future conquests at small, intimate dinner parties; personal introductions were ever so much nicer than the crude banalities of lesbian establishments. So far, her only "possibles" were that Erika Schultz woman, and a few other women she'd noted but hadn't met yet. Of course, there was that utterly smitten broad, whatsherface, the cruise coordinator. But she was simply too, too available – and that turned Lynn very, very off.

"Well, well, Miss Adler," a man's booming voice said, approaching. "Or do you prefer Ms.?"

She turned gracefully, a ready smile on her parted lips. "Why, Captain Margolies. How nice to see you." Her eyes assessed him from head to toe with indifferent inspection. For a man his age, he was in very good physical condition; a bit pudgy in the face, but his body was taut and trim. "Are you taking your constitutional?"

He laughed lightly. "No, I was just on my way to my quarters. But you didn't answer me – Miss or Ms.?"

Lynn tossed her long ash-blonde hair, letting the sea breeze play through it. "Either way. I'm not committed to labels."

His large hazel eyes became amused, a slightly flirtatious look in them. "I somehow got that feeling at dinner last evening. A young woman of your – shall we say – obvious loveliness should never lock herself into anything."

"Are you referring to the closet, captain?" she asked, toying with him, pleased to see his instant discomfort.

"No, not at all," he shot back, reddening. "Well, I'd better be going."

"See you at dinner," she called after him, then broke into a low, throaty and dirty laugh. After all, it wasn't every day that one could thoroughly embarrass the captain of a ship . . . and a ship's captain was like a nation's president

– he was Law while they were at sea. Yes, Lynn had enjoyed that. Even captains had to squirm once in awhile. ...

¤ ¤ ¤

Carmen Navasky hurried briskly toward Deck 4 and Dr. Amanda Holden's offices across from the purser's office. The telephone message on her desk had read "Important," and upon calling the ship's doctor, Amanda had filled her in briefly. It very much appeared that one of the passengers had measles. "Oh God," Carmen had groaned. "I'll be right there!"

She rounded the corner, nearly bumping into several middle-aged women dressed for a game of tennis or Ping-Pong, and mumbled an apology, trying not to let her genuine worry show in her brown eyes. Seconds later, she let herself into Amanda's office where the doctor was seated at her desk. "Measles?"

Amanda Holden looked up. "Is that a nickname, a greeting, or a question?"

"Please, Amanda, tell me you're wrong. I don't dare think what'll happen if the word gets around!"

"The *word*! What about the disease? It's highly contagious, Carmen. Don't you know that?"

"Yes, yes, of course. But after all, it's nothing terribly serious. I mean, didn't all of us have the measles when we were kids?"

"There are differences in medical thinking about any immunity that might provide," Amanda said quietly.

Carmen looked at her, trying to keep calm. A striking woman without being actually beautiful, Amanda Holden had never struck Carmen as an alarmist. Yet she seemed deadly earnest at the moment. Carmen studied the woman, seeking any sign of reassurance she might find.

But Amanda's thin face beneath the modified Afro was stoic, and her dark eyes revealed nothing. "All right," Carmen said at length, perching on the end of the desk. "Let's have it."

Putting on brass-rimmed reading glasses, Amanda opened a file folder before her. "The patient thought she was coming down with a cold three days ago."

"Before boarding?"

"Yes."

"That's a relief. At least she can't say she picked up the disease aboard the S.S. *Sisterhood*."

The doctor's lips parted in a sympathetic smile. "The usual symptoms: fever, sneezing, and a cough. Last night, though, she complained to her lover that her eyes were becoming terribly sensitive to light."

Carmen nodded. "How well I remember the drawn blinds and closed curtains of my childhood bedroom."

"Her eyes were pink from inflammation, and her face started to get puffy."

"Not just your common garden-variety cold," Carmen commented, sighing.

"No, and photophobia is no laughing matter when you're on a cruise in the Pacific . . . that sun glinting off the ocean could be highly dangerous."

"Amanda, please. Don't draw it all out. Just what should we do?"

She closed the folder and gazed at Carmen. "The rash started this morning. There's not a doubt in my mind, Carmen, she has measles." Leaning forward, she patted Carmen's hand. "The captain isn't going to like this, but we must get her ashore . . . if not to a hospital, then at least to a good hotel."

"Ashore! But *why*? Can't she and her lover just remain quarantined in their cabin?"

Amanda removed her glasses and rubbed her eyes thoughtfully. "It's not just contagion I'm worried about,

Carmen. One of the myths about measles that has been dispelled is that it's a mild disease, with little or nothing to worry about. Though it's not commonplace, measles can lead to ear infections, pneumonia, and there have been cases of permanent brain damage."

She rose and walked around to Carmen, putting her arm about her shoulder comfortingly. "Do we dare take that risk? My facilities here are very limited, and if she gets worse . . . or others contract it, well, we could be leaving ourselves wide open to a lawsuit."

Carmen glanced downward, just noticing that her hands were tightly clasped on her lap. It was a helluva situation! All those women bound and determined to have a wonderful holiday cruise to Mexico's Riviera . . . and now this! In the five years that she had worked on passenger liners, this was the very first time that she'd been confronted with an infectious disease. She supposed she should consider herself lucky, but Carmen didn't. Worse, this was the S.S. *Sisterhood*'s maiden cruise. Word of mouth could destroy any hopes for a subsequent voyage. Her shoulders rose and fell in resignation. "I guess we'll just have to tell the captain."

"Would you prefer that I do it?" Amanda asked solicitously.

"No, I'll tell him. Thanks anyway."

"Why don't I come with you, then. You know how he is."

Carmen snorted lightly. "Yes, I know what a sonuvabitch the pompous bastard can be. Okay, maybe you're right. At least you'll be there to back me up." She glanced up at Amanda then to the ceiling. "Why me, God? Why me?"

"Next time, you might try praying to the Goddess . . . your luck might improve," Amanda teased lightly. "Come on, let's go."

Carmen observed the doctor walk to the door and

pull it open, waiting quietly. "Why do I feel a firing squad coming on?"

Amanda laughed. "Drawn and quartered is the nautical punishment, I believe. Or is it keelhauled?"

"I don't know how you can be taking this so lightly," Carmen said, joining her to step over the threshold.

"I'm not taking it lightly," she contradicted amiably. "But whether the captain likes it or not, we're going to have to put in at Ensenada."

"What'll we tell the rest of the passengers?" Carmen asked, suddenly worried that the news might put a pall on the voyage.

"We'll think of something, Carmen. That's the least of our worries. First we've got to convince Captain Margolies that he has no choice but to put this woman ashore. Excuses can be made later."

"I only wish I could be as confident as you are."

Amanda pulled the door closed and locked it carefully, according to regulations. A ship's doctor's office was a natural target for anyone seeking a quick high and precautions were commensurately effected. "There's a great little *cantina* in Ensenada . . . I'll buy you a margarita to cheer you up."

"Oh God," Carmen said, covering her ears and rushing ahead, wanting to have this ordeal over with as quickly as possible. . . .

CHAPTER FIVE

THE TWO WOMEN FOUND the captain in the wheelhouse on the bridge deck, barking out a command to the young man at the gleaming brass helm. All Carmen could think about was the old movies on television about World War II, or the sinking of the *Titanic*. Surely the ship was in no danger from enemy submarines . . . much less an iceberg – so why was Captain Margolies shouting? But then, it was very like him. About five-foot-ten, with thinning light brown hair, his face showed all too clearly what and who he was.

Tanned – but an unhealthy color, as if applied with makeup – his face was full, though not fat, and revealed the tendency to overindulge in rich foods and expensive liquor. His hazel eyes were large, fringed with dark brown lashes – the sort of face one knew had once been beautiful as a child. His mouth was wide, with thin, sensual lips . . . perhaps a little cruel or sadistic; and Captain Margolies had kept himself in perfect trim, working out every day – which he bragged about at every opportunity.

Carmen had never liked him; but then, she didn't have to. She found him arrogant, overbearing, and the epitome of a man suffering from a Casanova complex. Although, admittedly, until this year when the shipping company had agreed to convert the craft for all-lesbian cruises, Captain Margolies had done very well in the romance department. Or, at least, so he claimed.

The feeling of dislike was mutual, Carmen knew. Ever since she had convinced the president of Ammex Lines, Inc., to cater to the lesbian market, the captain had hated her guts.

"Two weeks with a bunch of queers aboard? You're crazy!" he'd bellowed at the meeting. "I never thought that *you* would be interested in something like *that*!" He'd turned to the president and smirked. "Next she'll be telling us that she's some dyke!"

It had taken all of Carmen's determination not to succumb to his sneering derision. "I don't think that anyone's sexual preference is at issue," she'd said pointedly to the president. "The object is profits. We simply are not competing with the Princess Line; despite the fact that more and more people are taking cruises, we're losing our share of passengers."

"I agree, Miss Navasky," the president had said calmly, glaring at the captain. "But, well, the idea of an all-lesbian cruise – how would we advertise?"

Carmen had smiled. "The same as everyone else does, though admittedly, with some periodicals we may have to be circumspect."

"Circumspect!" Captain Margolies snarled.

"Go on, Miss Navasky. I'd like to hear more. It's a challenging idea, I must admit."

Carmen then reached down for her attaché case, put it on her lap, and opened it. Inside were months and months of careful preparation for that moment. "According to the outdated Kinsey Institute statistics, there are between two and eight million adult lesbians in this country alone."

Captain Margolies rolled his eyes upward. "What a damned loss!"

"To you personally, captain?" Carmen had asked demurely. He'd glowered at her, but made no response, so she resumed. "There are no valid studies done on disposable income for the lesbian segment, but we know they spend a great deal on vans, stereo equipment, chain saws, lawn mowers, and so forth. Not being saddled with families, their earnings are their own . . . not handed over to husbands or spent on new shoes for the kids."

"Good lord, this is insanity," Captain Margolies muttered.

By then, Carmen's temper was beginning to take over. "Are you being judgmental, captain? Or would you prefer to see Ammex Lines go into receivership? I won't have any trouble finding a job . . . but you might."

He'd leaned forward, scowling. "Meaning?"

Carmen smiled. "Meaning simply that there are only so many ships, and only one captain is required for each of them. The need for cruise coordinators, however, is substantial; besides, most of us can double in other capacities."

And so the meeting had gone, with the captain dickering and naysaying, pointing out that the ship's crew was all male and it could only lead to a lot of problems. However, in the end, common sense prevailed and the president had agreed to give the idea a trial run. Every possible post would be filled by women – if qualified – though obviously men would have to run the ship itself. Only, as he had quickly pointed out, because there were not accredited women to do so – at least, not yet.

That had been months ago and Captain Margolies had never reconciled himself to being captain of a shipful of lesbians. He was cordial in their midst, occasionally even courtly, but Carmen knew it ate at the man. This first cruise out, the passenger log was so small it hardly paid to hoist anchor. But Carmen knew it would become more and more talked about, and women would begin to book tickets from all over the nation. It would build into a good business for Ammex Lines, for travel agents – for hotels and tourist places as women made connecting arrangements – and it was good for lesbians.

So far, the only time Carmen had seen the captain even begin to show his seductive colors – since this cruise had begun – had been when Lynn Adler had appeared for dinner last night. His male ego had surfaced, his eyes feasting on Lynn; not that Carmen blamed him. Still, it was the first time since they set sail that he'd been more than politely gracious. Carmen had no doubt as to why.

Now, watching him in the wheelhouse, Carmen was glad that Amanda had come with her. "Captain Margolies?"

"What is it!" he growled irritably, turning to face them.

"We've a little problem," Carmen said cautiously.

"All women have 'little' problems!"

"Only in the eyes of 'little' men, captain," Amanda said, stepping forward, her dark eyes flashing. "Which, of course, we know you're not." She smiled faintly. "We have a sick patient aboard who has to be taken ashore. Now you can either arrange for a helicopter to come get her and her lover, or you can radio ahead that we're putting in at Ensenada."

"What? Who the hell do you think is in command of

this ship, you –"

He stopped himself, but Carmen knew Amanda had also seen the way his mouth had formed to say "black" – with whatever else he had intended to use after it. Bitch? Lesbian? Whore? It didn't matter. In his mouth, they were all the same.

Between them, it had taken a little more than fifteen minutes to convince him that the two passengers had to be removed from the ship. Since there was no way a helicopter could land on the vessel, the port of Ensenada was the only other choice. And if it hadn't been for Carmen sinking home that he would be liable in the event the passenger's condition worsened, he would never have agreed.

So it was settled that the best way to handle this diversion from schedule was to say there was some mechanical problem. It was far better than chancing lowered morale.

After they left the wheelhouse, standing just beyond the door, the two women exchanged relieved glances. "Thanks," Carmen said.

"My pleasure. When do you plan to make the announcement?"

"At the three seatings for lunch. Nobody ever misses lunch, right?" Carmen tried to look cheerful.

Amanda smiled knowingly. "You know, sometimes I think the only reason men think they can rule the world is because they have no grasp of what's wrong with it. Ignorance in thrashing action."

Carmen laughed briefly. "You have a damned good point."

¤ ¤ ¤

Donna and Sandy stood by the railing, arms about each other's waists, with Sandy resting her head against her lover's shoulder. "It sure looks different from here, doesn't it, darling?"

Donna nodded. "Driving the camper, those low chaparral-covered hills look like an abandoned planet. From here on the ship, with the sea in between, there's kind of a majesty about it. Don't you think?"

Sandy squeezed Donna harder. "You're such a romantic. I'll bet no one knows that about you except me."

"Romantic? Who, me?" Donna grinned. "What makes you say that?"

She looked up, her blue eyes twinkling affectionately. "Words like 'majestic' and 'abandoned planet,' " Sandy pointed out. "You're all the time coming up with stuff like that. Maybe you should try to write a book, Donna."

"Oh sure. Maybe when I retire. I'll write a lesbian novel – how's that?" she asked playfully.

"You wouldn't, would you?"

"Why not? Maybe a science-fiction one – that would be fun. A world that's run by women. What do you think?"

"Isn't that what the Amazons did?"

"Were they lesbians?"

"I don't know."

Just then, Mac and Carol came toward them. "Hi. Are you goin' ashore?"

"Does anybody know how long we'll be in port?" Sandy asked, her left hand tracing light circles on Donna's back.

Carol smoothed her broad-striped moo-moo then smiled at Donna, but her eyes belied it. "Don't make much difference. I'm not lettin' Mac go anywhere till she wins back some of the money you've taken off her."

"Aw, come on," Donna said, not certain just how serious Carol was. Although they were just friendly poker games, it wouldn't be the first time that somebody's lover got uptight about losses. "I'll probably lose my shirt tomorrow."

"And I'm Jane Fonda," Carol said tightly.

"Knock it off, Carol," Mac said, her thin mouth showing her discomfort as she scratched at her face. "It was just one afternoon's game, for crissakes. You gonna ruin this whole trip just because of *that*?"

"You got any bread left on you, bigshot?"

Donna felt miserably uncomfortable. Was Carol just going out of her way to punish her lover, or had Mac really lost all she had? There was no way that Donna wanted to make anyone upset about a little poker game; but on the other hand, if Mac didn't have the money to play, she should've stayed out of the game. Worse, if she were to offer to give back the money, it could only put Mac in a humiliating position. Donna had never come up against a situation like this before. She looked down at Sandy in hopes of picking up some kind of a hint of what to do, but Sandy's light eyes showed she was just as confused and embarrassed as Donna was.

Then, as if the full implication were sinking in, Sandy drew herself up to her full five-foot-two and squared her shoulders. Her eyes narrowed as the color slowly left her face. "Are you saying what I *think* you are?" she challenged Carol's hulk.

"Why honey, whatever do you mean?" Carol asked, her lips curled sarcastically.

"Because if you are. . . . " Sandy leaned forward as if to leap at the huge woman, but Donna placed her hand on Sandy's shoulder.

"Take it easy, hon."

Sandy looked up, cold fury in her blue eyes. "Easy! Don't you see what she's driving at? She's got the . . . the *gall* to suggest you were cheating!"

"I didn't say that," Carol replied with bovine coyness, "you did."

"Let me at her," Sandy hissed, trying to wrestle free from Donna's grip.

"Hey, now look," Mac said sternly, turning to Carol.

You're way out of line! Ain't no way Donna could've rigged that hand. She won fair an' square. So knock it off, Big Mamma!"

"Thanks, Mac," Donna said, relieved. However, she was not about to let go of Sandy's shoulder. She knew her too well, and when Sandy got angry – which was seldom – she could fight her weight in wildcats. There were only two things that Donna had ever seen Sandy get fighting mad over: one was being talked down to; and the other was to be falsely accused . . . which spilled over into a protective stance for Donna as well. Things that Donna would probably never even notice – or even if she did, would tend to let go – Sandy would rise up to defend. She was little, but Donna had never known her to take any guff from anybody.

While Carol didn't actually cower at Mac's directive, her visage revealed that she knew she'd gone too far. However, by then, many of the other passengers had gone to that side of the ship to see where they were headed. Pinky and her lover, Olga, were among them, and Donna was genuinely glad to see them. Despite short acquaintance, Pinky had demonstrated herself to be something of a whiner and a poor loser – poker revealed many things about people; but Olga was totally different. Though she also was overweight, next to Carol she looked sylphlike; but more importantly, Olga was one of those women who took it upon herself to mother everyone else along. She seemed genial, laughed a great deal, and if anything really bothered her, so far Olga hadn't let it show.

"Hi, you two," Donna greeted, perhaps a little too effusively.

Pinky's wiry frame edged its way to the ship's railing. "Looks like some kind of Alcatraz or somethin'. Ain't a green patch nowheres."

Still bristling, Sandy took advantage of the break in mood and headed toward Pinky, passing Carol as if the woman didn't exist. "You should see it inland, though," she said, pretending nothing had happened moments before. "Once you get between there and El Rosario, there are these really weird trees called cirio, and huge cardons . . . it's really beautiful."

Smiling, Donna looked down at Olga. "Sandy can find something good in anything," she said appreciatively.

Olga's droopy brown eyes showed her agreement as Carol and Mac joined the other two at the railing. "Feels a bit tense around here," Olga said. "Anything wrong?"

Surprised, Donna shook her head. "Why, no. Why do you ask?"

Olga smiled secretively. "I don't claim to be a psychic or anything, but I'm pretty good at picking up vibrations. I'd say something was going on just before Pinky and I showed up."

Donna sighed. "Well, there was a bit of a tiff. Carol was sort of in left field."

"Watch out for her," Olga advised quietly. "She could be very dangerous."

"Dangerous?"

Nodding, Olga explained: "She's mean . . . mean inside. Carol hates herself so much she can't stand to see anyone else having a good time or being happy."

"How do you know that?" Donna asked, not knowing whether to believe her or not.

Olga tilted her head sideways, her sleepy brown eyes veiled. "I've seen her kind before."

Donna grinned. "I think that's called a sweeping assertion, isn't it?"

"How old are you, Donna?"

"Forty. Why?"

"Give yourself another ten years. When you reach my age, you'll find out that the sweeping assertions of ten years ago are, in all likelihood, the truths of today."

Donna laughed. "How can you say that? You might

as well tell me that all blondes are innocent and all brunettes are evil."

Olga smiled. "Let me put it this way, then. We're all the products of what's inside of us, and as we get older, it begins to show on our faces. Are the frown lines from worry or constant disapproval, are the lips tight and compressed or quick to smile . . . if you pay attention, it isn't too hard to 'read' what somebody is. Of course, you've got to keep an open mind . . . there's always the margin for error. It could all be from poor health or constant pain."

"But you're pretty sure about Carol, aren't you," Donna asked, beginning to take Olga seriously.

"Yes. If nothing else, listen to her voice. It's high-pitched and shrill, tight and grating . . . not the voice of someone who's comfortable with herself, but instead, in constant inner turmoil."

"Where did you learn all of this?" Donna asked, only half in joking.

"By being alive long enough."

"No, come on. Really."

"All right," Olga conceded. "I'm a clinical psychologist. There have been signs about a person's self-image long before there were books about body language. Couple that with all the years of counseling I've done . . . and yes, you get to be pretty good at sizing people up."

The corners of Donna's mouth turned down as she accepted that Olga's education and experience probably would give her an edge in knowing what to expect from people. She turned to seek out Sandy, but by now there were entirely too many people. At only five-foot-two, it was very easy to lose Sandy in a crowd. However, emerging like the waterboy from between the warriors, Sandy soon appeared with a very chic woman in tow. Donna knew that they'd met, but couldn't quite place where.

"Darling. Look who I've found."

Donna struggled to remember the woman's name

but only drew a blank. "Hi," she said blithely, hoping her broad smile would hide the truth.

"It's nice to see you again, Donna," the woman said, her oval face framed by short, curly dark brown hair.

"Uh, thanks." Dammit all! What was her name!

"Felice Capezio," she volunteered.

Her grin widened. "Oh, I remembered your name," Donna lied, hoping that the flush she felt on her neck didn't show.

"Felice is going ashore," Sandy said animatedly.

"Why not? Carmen said that we'd be here until at least five or six o'clock this evening. I've never been to Ensenada, so I may as well take advantage of it."

"Well then, why don't we go together?" Sandy put in excitedly. "We've been here maybe four or five times, so we can show you around."

Felice didn't respond right away, and Donna thought she knew why. "Maybe Felice made arrangements to go with someone else," she said, giving the younger woman an out. Felice wasn't part of their set, and Donna knew it. She belonged with those others, the ones who wore lipstick and mascara; who, even in jeans and a sweatshirt, would still look totally chic and worldly. Donna didn't mind, actually; she was simply being sensitive to Felice's feelings.

Felice turned large, lovely brown eyes on Donna, an impish look in them that said she appreciated Donna's thoughtfulness, but that it was unnecessary. "No, I didn't make plans," she said with gracious uncertainty, as if she feared she might have offended Donna. "I was just going to explore on my own."

"Then, c'mon, let's all go together," Sandy insisted, tugging at Donna's sleeve with a jerk of her head toward Mac and Carol. "Let's get out of here while the goin's good," she added in a whisper.

Catching on, Donna nodded like the chairperson of the board approving a merger. "We'd better hurry, then. Let's get our stuff and meet at the tour desk in ten minutes."

"Where's that?" Felice asked, a silly look of confused anticipation on her face.

"Deck 6, where the gangplank is," Sandy answered as she pulled Donna away from the crowd at the railing. "Ten minutes!"

"I'll be there," Felice called with a little wave.

¤ ¤ ¤

"*Yo soy como un chile verde, llorona, picante pero sabroso! Ay de mi llorona. . . .*" The three mariachi players strolled away, and Felice could only stare at the backs of their worn, frayed bolero jackets, wishing they'd come back. She'd heard records of Mexican mariachis before, but she'd never dreamed that their music could be like this! A guitarist, another with a twelve-string guitar that Donna had called a *guitarrón*, and a cornet player. That was all. Loud, sometimes off key, but with a haunting, plaintive sound that Felice doubted she would ever forget. For a little while, a beggar with a squeaky violin had come into the *cantina*, playing along while a shaggy yellow dog waited in the doorway. However, the "official" mariachis had scowled him away after he'd passed his battered *sombrero* to a few of the customers – obviously, cutting in on what the others would get in tips. Making short, quick bows, smiling with missing teeth, the beggar had practically backed out of the place and left with a tail-wagging dog on his heels.

Sandy leaned across the initial-scarred table toward Felice. "Isn' it won'erful?" she asked, slurring happily.

Felice tried to nod but her head felt wooden. "'S

beautiful," she managed . . . barely.

Donna's pale blue eyes looked at the two of them with obvious difficulty in focusing. "Anybody wan' 'nother margarita?" She tried to hide a hiccup but didn't succeed.

"Sure," Sandy drawled out as if agreeing to the obvious.

The mariachis struck up a lively tempo and began to sing "Guadalajara" with more gusto than talent. The cornetist was particularly in his element and with the instrument to his lips, his eyes gleamed merrily. Felice sat back against her chair, feeling the music right from the floorboards up to her torso, unable to stop herself from tapping her foot with an inanely pleased expression. She knew her eyebrows were going up and down with the music, but that seemed perfectly all right to her.

"Hey, Fel," Donna said, swaying slightly on her chair. "You wan' another?"

"How many have I had?" Felice asked clinically.

Donna frowned, holding up her hand and counting off on her fingers. "Three . . . four. . . ." Donna shrugged helplessly, saying: "Who cares?"

Felice smiled. How great it was not to care. No place she had to be; no race for work in the morning. She nodded just because that's what she felt like doing at the moment. Then she glanced around the battered old saloon as if wanting to memorize every detail. The place was filled mostly with tourists – she could tell by the way they were dressed in floral prints and Bermuda shorts or cutoffs; most of them laden with purchases in bags or boxes. At the long bar, numerous men were seated nursing beers or tall, cool drinks. They looked like Americans, though it was hard to tell for sure. They all had a sort of down-at-the-heels appearance, as if having given up on life due to some sort of personal tragedy. Not bums, actually; just down on their luck or indifferent. Behind the bar were scores of eight-by-ten-inch black-and-white photographs, framed; it was too far away for Felice to be able to discern who the subjects were.

A man with a shoeshine box ambled into the *cantina*, pausing at each table expectantly; then an old woman entered, selling paper flowers.

Suddenly, Donna's arm shot straight up, with her hand dangling and circling over the three of them as if putting a curse on them. Felice glanced over at her, wondering what kind of a spasm she was suffering from, until she saw a waiter nod at them and move toward the bartender. *We're going to have another margarita,* she thought with dulled alarm. *My God, we're going to have another! Well, if they can walk out of here, so can I! It's my* vacation . . . *my first trip out of the country!*

Even though seated, she felt her body swaying and concentrated on holding it very, very still. *Like a little mousey*, she told herself, pretending there was a big cat watching her. "Shh, little mousey."

"Wha'?"

Felice looked at Sandy. Nice Sandy. Really rather pretty. "Wha'?"

"You say somethin'?"

"Me?" Felice laughed to herself. "No. It was my frien', the mousey."

"Who?" Donna leaned forward, nearly tipping over her glass.

The waiter arrived just in time, clearing away the empty cocktail glasses, emptying the filled ashtray, and wiping the table meticulously. "You are 'aving a nice time, *señoritas*?" he asked pleasantly, putting down the fresh drinks.

"Won'erful," Sandy said just as the mariachis stopped playing and began to stroll about the room with their *sombreros* upturned.

"Why'd they stop?" Felice asked, her feelings hurt.

"They go on now, *señorita*, to another *cantina*. It is 'ow they make their living – *sí*?"

Donna pulled out a man's billfold, shaking her head as if she'd just been challenged. "Now, this one's on me." She pulled out a twenty-dollar bill and dropped it onto the waiter's tray. "Keep the change," she instructed, her chin tucked in smugly.

"But *señorita*, this is too much," the waiter protested.

"Found money," she said airily. "I won it at poker."

The waiter looked from Sandy to Felice, perplexed.

Felice lifted her shoulders indifferently, and Sandy stared at the bill fixedly, then smiled contentedly. "It's her money," she responded with profundity.

"*Gracias, señorita, gracias,*" he said with incredulous elation, then left them as if fearing Donna would change her mind.

A shadow blocked the main entrance and Felice turned her head in the general direction, though with the sunlight behind the person, she couldn't see the face. However, whomever it was, the approach to their table was with a firm step. *Sober*, Felice observed silently, wondering why anyone would be sober on such a beautiful afternoon. She attempted a welcoming smile.

"So this is where you are."

Felice looked up to see Carmen Navasky's tanned attractive face. Her expression was amused, but she had the aura of someone on a mission about her – like a Collie rounding up sheep. "Bark, bark," Felice greeted, then laughed at her own joke.

Carmen smiled tolerantly. "Perhaps you three don't know it, but our ship is leaving in forty-five minutes. You'd better get a taxi, considering the shape you're in."

Donna bent toward Sandy. "Is she insulting us?"

Sandy shook her head. "She's smiling . . . see? But I think she thinks we're drunk."

"A roadie," Felice said, lifting her glass.

"You don't really have time for one for the road," Carmen explained in a calm, quiet voice. "You don't want to spend your whole vacation in Ensenada, do you?"

That sounded all right to Felice; why not? She was having a great time; what difference did it make if it was aboard the S.S. *Sisterhood* or right here in Ensenada? Silly question when you got right down to it.

". . . I'm still missing three others, so I can't stay. Sandy, can I put you in charge?"

" 'Five-foot-two, eyes of blue, she's my. . . .' "

"All right. Then you, Donna. You're with L.A.'s finest, and you're the biggest. Can I trust you to get these two back to the ship?"

Donna straightened, her light blue eyes staring fixedly. "Yessir! You can rely on me!"

Carmen snorted good-naturedly. "It's up to you three. The ship won't wait for you."

"Who else is missin'?" Sandy asked as if checking her guest list.

"A couple from Cabin 448, and . . . one other."

"Who," Sandy demanded lightly.

"Get back to the ship and I'll tell you," Carmen said, then quickly took her leave.

¤ ¤ ¤

The sun looked unreal as it hovered over the horizon, sending golden ripples across the bay as the ship slowly pulled out. Though they could have gotten the sick passenger and her lover onto shore in a matter of half an hour or less, Carmen and Captain Margolies had finally agreed it would be better to take the entire day. It would mean increasing the knots between ports, but it was better than having the passengers become suspicious about their detour to Ensenada. Instead, they could go shopping or even fishing, believing only that the ship had needed some minor repairs. Even the most fun-filled cruise could get repetitious, so the chance to disembark and be on dry land would be wiser than a quick stop without letting the passengers off the ship.

And judging from the way some of them had returned to the S.S. *Sisterhood*, many were feeling no pain. At least, Carmen reflected while standing at the porthole of her stateroom, Felice and the other two had made it back safely. She'd had some grave doubts back at Hussong's *cantina*. Then she laughed. Obviously, Felice was not accustomed to hard liquor – certainly not tequila. Carmen knew all too well how frequently passengers landed in Mexico, downing those lethal margaritas as if they were lemonades; more than one woman had slid off a barstool, never knowing what had happened!

But at least Felice was a happy drunk; she had to give her that. "Bark, bark," she mimicked aloud, shaking her head.

Then she became more serious. The passengers from Cabin 448 had finally shown up, blitzed to the core. Well, they were young. Carmen figured them to be perhaps, at most, twenty-two or so.

However, Lynn Adler was still missing. She'd taken off by herself, so there was no way that Carmen could make even discreet inquiries about where she might have gone. And though Carmen had checked every bar, saloon, *cantina*, and restaurant, there was no sign of Lynn Adler. It would have been easy to miss her, of course. Since Ensenada was dependent upon the tourists for its meager income – other than their fishing industry and the nearby Santo Tomás Winery – bars were everywhere. She could easily have been just one saloon behind Lynn and never have known it. Yet, somehow Lynn didn't strike her as the type of woman who would go in for that kind of entertainment. She was far too cool, too in control of herself for that type of indulgence.

Maybe she'd taken a long walk on the beach, stretched out, and fallen asleep. Or perhaps she'd gone shopping for the colorful and inexpensive earthenware made right at the numerous sidewalk shops. Or even the few stores that catered to the affluent, offering French perfumes and pure cashmere sweaters, imported woolens and fine china or crystal . . . all at significant savings over U.S. prices – yes, Carmen could envision Lynn trying on dress after dress. It would fit the picture she had of the stunning young woman. And she cursed herself for not having thought to look in these places for Lynn. Of course, she was confident that Lynn could take care of herself. She'd probably charter a flight in the morning and meet the ship at Mazatlán, enjoying a few more days than the others had to wander around.

Glancing at her watch, Carmen wondered just how many of today's revelers would make it for the first dinner seating – or even the second. Some of them were probably sleeping it off even then.

She started as her telephone rang unexpectedly.

Stretching across her bunk, Carmen lifted the receiver. "Hello?"

"Hi, it's Amanda."

"What's up?" she asked with guarded interest.

"Just a follow-up report. You might want to tell the captain what's happened with our patient."

"Dare I ask?"

"I got her to a hotel, with her lover's help, and explained to the hotel doctor what the problem was. He was sympathetic, but unhappy."

"I'll bet," Carmen replied with a little laugh. No one in the tourist business ever wanted to contend with sick people.

"Well, I telephoned him just before we pulled out."

"And?"

"The patient and her lover had a terrible quarrel, the patient checked out of the hotel, and as far as we know took a charter plane back to L.A."

Carmen rolled over onto her elbows, frowning slightly. "Are we liable for that?"

"I shouldn't think so."

"What happened to her lover?"

"Beats me."

"She's not checked off the manifest, only the patient was. I looked that over very carefully before we set sail from Ensenada." Carmen took in her stateroom absently, enjoying the way the setting sun turned everything golden, like lost treasures from the Mayan pyramids.

"Anyway, thought you'd like to have the update. It might be best to tell the captain before he finds out in some other way. He'll have our necks on a chopping block if he thinks we put into Ensenada for nothing."

"Did the Mexican doctor concur with your diagnosis?"

Amanda laughed. "Of course."

"Then I don't think we have anything to worry about. But thanks for telling me."

"Sure. See you later," Amanda said. "We may be the only two women at dinner tonight."

Carmen smiled. "No, though I'll grant you, lots of them were pretty high. But many passengers stayed aboard, and there was a fair showing of P&Ps."

"P&Ps?"

"Prim and Proper."

"I'll remember that," Amanda said, then hung up.

Carmen replaced the receiver, wondering if they could get into any trouble because Ms. Shapiro had flown on to Los Angeles. She doubted it, but still. . . . And too, what had happened to her lover, Ms. O'Shea? Had she stayed on in Ensenada? Could Ammex be held responsible if anything happened to her while there?

Then suddenly, she became aware that the ship's engines had slowed to a neutral. Kneeling, she glanced out her porthole. The sea was quiet, shimmering in orange-gold and blue with silvery caps glinting like Fourth of July sparklers against the rapidly approaching dusk. The ship wasn't moving at all. *What's going on*? she asked herself, getting down from her bunk. Hastily, she stepped to the mirror to be sure her makeup was all right, then ran a comb through her dark brown hair. Slipping out to the passageway, Carmen swiftly made her way past the telephone center to the tour desk, then turned right at the broad hallway that led to the elevators that would take her up to the Promenade Deck.

Wishing she'd brought a sweater, she semi-trotted to the starboard and looked out. Heading toward the ship at a goodly clip was a private motor launch. Berating herself for being too vain to wear her distance glasses, Carmen had to wait for the launch to come alongside. There, bobbing gently, the launch waited while two women – huddled together – were thrown a rope ladder. They were shivering but laughing and Carmen gasped when they were close enough to recognize. Ms. O'Shea . . . and Lynn Adler! Disheveled, they had the look of . . . of *lovers*! Had they found each other at the hotel and . . .? Lynn Adler with Ms. O'Shea? The flat-chested, nondescript Marsha O'Shea? *Oh no!*

CHAPTER SIX

ERIKA AND CHARLENE'S CABIN, No. 42, was the very first one on the port side of Deck 4, three tiers beneath the bridge deck and in a direct line under the wheelhouse. The cabin occupied by Shapiro and O'Shea was midship on the same deck, aft of the purser's office, information desk, elevators, and Amanda Holden's offices.

Charlene had insisted that Erika take advantage of the layover in Ensenada to get some serious work done – or else. While Erika had pretended to be annoyed, she was more than glad. In her heyday, she had been to Ensenada more times than she cared to remember, and knew Baja California probably better than Manhattan; if that was possible. However, back then, Erika had thought nothing of chartering private planes to take her – and her current flame – to Baja California for the weekend . . . especially in winter. At that time, tourists were few and far between, and one could rent a small villa for next to nothing. Balmy days, watching sunsets on the ocean beyond sentinels of palm trees, listening to soft Mexican music drifting from God-knew-where, and service that had no equal for sincerity and warm graciousness, Ensenada was an unspoiled paradise.

In the early 1950s, it was Tijuana that took the brunt of American tourists – mostly because of the bullring and the then famous Caesar's Hotel, which took credit as the home of the Caesar salad and popularizer of margaritas to martini-bored patrons. How long ago that all seemed to Erika now. How many times in the last six years had she felt as if she were two people: one who had been young and wild, free-spending, able to capture any woman of her choice with a winning smile; and now, the puppet at the end of Charlene's choke collar. She remembered all the details of that other life vividly, yet it was as if she were privy to a complete dossier of someone else. When was she an imposter? Then, or now? Certainly, the person she had been in the past bore no relationship to her present existence. Did she need a lovely princess to awaken her, to bring her back to reality? Or was it too late. . . .

Still, despite Charlene's irksome "command," Erika realized that it would be a perfect day to get some real work done. She didn't know how other writers scheduled themselves; only that for her, the best way was to get a couple of days' running start at a book. It was, for her, rather like trying to quit smoking or drinking. That first twenty-four hours' commitment was the beginning; if you could hang in for another twenty-four hours, you knew you'd live through it. And once a week or two had gone by, you were on pretty firm ground; smug, and bolstered enough to stick it out.

THE CRUISE

Though Charlene's idea about finishing the book during the cruise had sounded sensible in principle – no phone calls, no drop-ins, no errands to be run – it hadn't worked thus far. She had traded one set of distractions, or excuses, for another. Though, granted, this was only the third day of the voyage. Erika had long ago learned that to force herself to do something was to waste her time; doing what she didn't want to do only resulted in poor performance. Not that Charlene could ever understand that! Charlene's mind worked like a metronome and she never could comprehend why everyone else's didn't also. There was no room in her mind for moods, inspiration from the muses, upsets, spring fever, or any other interruption from the schedule of the day.

However, Erika had put in a good day's work at the typewriter after rereading what she had already written. She'd already covered the Jim Jones tragedy, getting it out of the way early simply because it was a fait accompli; unlike Rev. Sun Myung Moon's Unification Church and its constant problems with lawsuits that required updating lest the book be old-hat before it was even published. Erika had also covered groups such as the Subud and Meher Baba – not because nothing would change, but because, compared to some, they were almost harmless.

The others, or at least many of them, worried Erika more than she knew how to admit and the trick was to keep her genuine disapproval out of the body of her book. When she spoke to followers of the New Testament Missionary Fellowship, the Church of Scientology, or the Anand Marg . . . Erika had truly begun to worry about the mind-controlling manifestations. From Hare Krishna to Brother Julius, to the Church of Satan, hundreds of thousands of young Americans were dropping out from traditional society, turning their lives inside out, abandoning educations or careers . . . all in pursuit of spiritual freedom from the shackles of materialism. When questioned about the fact that so many of their "leaders" drove Rolls Royces, lived on palatial estates, invested lavishly in commercial property or potentially high-income stocks or bonds, Erika never ceased to be amazed at the rabid way the followers would defend their leaders. It simply was impossible to get through to them that if the object is spiritual freedom, divorce from materialism, then the heads of these cults were walking lies. Every kid she talked to had a programmed, perfect comeback – at least for the speaker, if not in Socratic methodology.

And it was here that Erika knew she was out of her depth. To write this book effectively, one *had* to have the academic background from which to glean valid arguments with which to counter the glib assertions of mindless devotion. It was not enough to disapprove or to care; she was unable to spontaneously rebut, based on her own education and experience. And how Charlene had ever sold the outline and sample chapters to a publisher was a miracle to Erika. Except that it was now up to Erika to perform a feat that Charlene seemed to equate with writing a recipe.

Later, as they rode down the aft set of elevators, just before the lounge for playing cards or pool, Erika was pleased with her day's output. And perhaps because of it, even Charlene seemed to be in an improved mood.

They entered the dining room on Deck 6 with Charlene preceding . . . like a quarter note before Erika's five-foot-nine arpeggio of confidence.

She turned around and looked up at Erika accusatorily. "I know we're early, but there aren't even half the diners there should be!"

Erika shrugged, her cashmere blazer's silk lining swooshing softly with the movement. "Maybe they all had dinner in town – or are just having a light snack at one of the cafes aboard."

"How can we be expected to have a pleasant dinner, with interesting conversation, if there's no one here?"

Charlene spun around, her chubby short arm indicating the numerous empty tables. "Of course, there really aren't all that many really interesting people aboard anyhow. Bunch of Yucca Valley hicks with their brains stuck in their twin cams!"

"C'mon, Charlene, that's no way to talk. You're going by your preconceived notions of appearances – and if that's the only criteria," Erika added with a lighthearted laugh, "then you leave yourself open to the same criticism."

Charlene's head snapped upward, her flattop hairdo tousled with the motion. "What's that supposed to mean?" she demanded, her voice going higher.

"Never mind," Erika said. "But if it's someone to talk to you want, how about over there? They look like a lively bunch. Assigned seating probably doesn't matter tonight."

Charlene followed the direction Erika had indicated with a nod of her head. "Well. . . ."

"They seem to have a great deal to say to each other," Erika prompted, yet knowing better than to lead the way. Charlene would decide where they would sit – just as she decided everything else in their lives.

"Let's give it a few minutes more," Charlene replied, tight-lipped. "Maybe some others will still drift in."

"Want to sit at our regular table in the meantime?"

"If I wanted to do that, I'd be doing it! Can't you just wait a little bit? I should think you'd be tired of sitting . . . that's all you've done for the entire day!"

"Oh for Pete's sake, Charlene," Erika muttered. "I was sitting because I was working! It's damned hard to type when swinging from a monkey rope!"

Charlene shifted her shoulders like a bird arranging its feathers in fussy display. "Did I say you weren't working? Why are you so touchy this evening?"

"Touchy!" She opened her mouth to say more, then

noted the closed door behind Charlene's hazel eyes. It would be pointless. As far as Charlene was concerned, there was nothing more to discuss.

"Oh look, here comes a nice-looking group of women. Let's see where they're sitting."

Erika shoved her hands into her pockets, saying nothing. However, she had to concur with Charlene's assessment. They seemed in their early or mid-thirties, had the aura of urbanites, and looked as if they could engage in diverting conversation. Erika tried not to notice the way Charlene was drinking them in. She looked like an over-the-hill courtesan trying to win a new lover . . . despite the odds against it. It embarrassed Erika. Charlene was always so pathetically *obvious*! If someone mentioned that she'd gone to NYU, Charlene would give a nausea-provoking smile and mumble "How nice," or something similar. But if anyone stated that she'd gone to Radcliffe, or any of the other Seven Sister schools, Charlene was all over them like a cheap suit, fawningly obsequious.

She recalled one summer, a few years before, when they had taken a house in the country. Erika stayed up there most of the time, while Charlene came up only for weekends. Erika had met a lesbian couple, both of whom were writers – published ones, not dilettantes – and had suggested to Charlene that they invite the two women over for cocktails and dinner. "They're very nice," Erika had said, smiling to herself with the glow of making friends in so rural an area. "You'd like them."

"Are they agented?"

"How the hell would I know?" Erika had responded.

"Look, Erika, I deal with crazy writers all week long. I'm sick to death of their bitching, always trying to hit me up for a loan, missing deadlines, bleeding over any suggestions for change! I'm a literary agent! I *know* what will sell and what won't!"

Erika had had to struggle to keep her temper in line.

"I thought agents agented, and editors asked for revisions – after all, it's the editor who has to be pleased, not you."

Charlene had sniffed in derision. "That's the Old Guard, Erika. You're behind the times. If these two creeps aren't agented, then invite them over. At least it'll be a tax deduction. Otherwise, forget it."

Erika had slumped with frustration. "What do you expect me to do? Call them up and say they're invited provided they need literary representation? Otherwise, stay home?"

"I don't care how you phrase it, Erika. All I'm saying is that I'm not wasting good booze on a couple of bull-dykes who don't have the sense to live in New York, where the action is."

She took a deep breath, counting to ten. "One, they're *not* bulldykes; and two, not everyone wants to live in the filth and crime-ridden atmosphere of your damned precious Manhattan!"

Charlene had looked at her like a naive child. "Then see them during the week, when I'm not around. And spend your *own* money to entertain them!"

As it later developed, the younger of the two had gone to only the best schools. When Erika happened to mention this to Charlene weeks later, her entire attitude had changed. "Why didn't you say so! That's different, Erika."

"But *why*? What makes it different?"

"That at least one of them is a person of taste and breeding. Obviously, she wouldn't be living with a total clod. Why not invite them over for drinks next Saturday?"

"Charlene," Erika had said slowly, baffled by the strange machinations of the other woman's mind, "what is this thing you have about where someone went to school? I didn't even go to college, but that never seemed to matter to you when we were going together."

"That was different."

"How?"

"You were a legend in your own time. These other . . . women," she said, using the word as if it caused the painful embarrassment of psoriasis, "are lesbians!"

"Good grief, Charlene! What are we? Martians?"

Charlene, thinner then, lifted her chin imperiously. "You're a lesbian, Erika. I'm not. I may find myself attracted to a woman from time to time, but it's not the same as being a real lesbian."

"It isn't?" Erika could only stare at her, dumbfounded.

"Of course not. You're dedicated, a confirmed lover of women. Whereas I am more inclined to a spiritual relationship."

"Hogwash!" Erika was really getting angry by then. "What about the women you've been seeing on the side? Don't you think I *know* about them? 'Yes, Erika, you may come into the city this weekend . . . I'm going to the country. No, Erika you can't stay in the apartment next Wednesday. . . . 'Do you honestly think I don't know what's been going on?"

Charlene blushed awkwardly then turned on her. "Well, if you've known, why haven't you said anything?"

"What for? You're calling the shots, not me."

"Don't you *care* that I'm seeing other women?"

"What for? Did you think I'd be jealous? Was that it?"

"I didn't think you'd find out," Charlene whimpered, her entire attitude changing as suddenly as a whirlwind dissipating, making one question that it had ever existed. "I never went to bed with any of them. . . . I swear! I . . . I do love you, Erika."

"Do you," she'd drawled out, hating the obvious lie of it, the hypocrisy. Erika had tried to be in love with Charlene, but she'd given up the pretense long ago. It hadn't been love; it had been desperation, loneliness, fear – but not love. Charlene was incapable of anything other than destruction; even of the things she cherished the most. And there was precious little of that. Her game was to humiliate and manipulate; to surround herself with people who would make her seem more important, more socially acceptable – but she didn't give a tinker's damn about anyone or anything other than herself and the "image" she allegedly created. Erika had long since put aside any illusions about their "relationship."

And now, Charlene was still up to her old tricks. Eying the six women as they sauntered toward a table at the far end of the dining room; looking for all the world like an eagle with a faded blonde wig, about to swoop on its prey. "Well?" Erika asked, not too patiently.

"I think they'll do," Charlene replied, arranging a convivial smile for their benefit.

"You think they'll do," Erika repeated, shaking her head.

⌑ ⌑ ⌑

The Mazatlán Ballroom was decorated in a combination of traditional American Christmas displays, combined with the colorful and picturesque Mexican artifacts of *posada.* Santa Claus and the Three Wise Men coexisted with Christmas trees and *piñatas*; glittering ornaments, tinsel, and blinking lights blended in with crèches and hand-painted Mexican doves of peace. It was a bizarre mixture, yet it seemed to work.

THE CRUISE

And Deck 3 that night was alive with passengers bent on having a good time. It was Christmas Eve. Felice stood with Carmen Navasky and Donna and Sandy – with whom she'd become rather good friends since their escapade in Ensenada. As Felice was fond of saying: "If you're good enough to get drunk with, you're good enough to be my friends." And she would always laugh after making that announcement. To her, what it really meant was that if she trusted someone enough to make a fool of herself, surely she could trust that person in other ways as well. And tonight she was working her way through the champagne with happy determination.

Actually, she had come to know Donna and Sandy pretty well since that afternoon. They were not particularly complicated women such as Felice had become accustomed to in New York. They didn't seem to have any grave hangups; in fact, they were very live-and-let-live in their attitudes. Sandy was by far the more outgoing and vivacious; but there was a dear, sweet quality to Donna too. Granted, Felice didn't know anything about life in Los Angeles, or how much fun it might be to take the camper out for weekends or vacations, but she could appreciate that their way of life didn't have to be the same as hers. For that matter, what was so wonderful about her life in the first place? Get up, go to work, come home. Sometimes go to a movie with Ann, or out to dinner. Occasionally, when the boredom was more than she could stand, call up a couple of gay guys she knew and hit the bars or go dancing.

Felice had married at the age of eighteen, a virgin, and never suspecting that she might be a lesbian. With all the wisdom of hindsight, Felice knew that she'd married simply because it was expected of her, and Doug had seemed a nice enough fellow. He was kind to her, brought her flowers before every date, and her folks approved of him. She'd gone all through high school with Doug, dating no one else, and it had sort of just fallen into place – Felice would marry him, and that was that. In Guttenburg, New Jersey, life pretty much followed a pattern. She and Doug would go to a movie, have a hamburger and a malted, then in his 1962 Chevy, they'd drive over to the cliffs overlooking the Hudson River. He'd put his arm around her shoulder dreamily while she stared at the incredible Manhattan skyline, wondering about all the people who lived there. They'd neck for a while, but Doug never pushed her to go all the way. Back then, Felice had often wondered what he'd done with his hard-on after each of those sessions.

When they were married, she soon learned why it was that Doug used to get out of the car before driving her home again. At the time, she had thought he simply wanted to empty his bladder. However, she quickly found out that Doug was a premature ejaculator. All he had to do after a date was touch himself to go off like a shooting rocket. Which did nothing to enhance their sex life. About eight months later, confused and worried that there was something wrong with her, Felice had confided to a friend of her mother's. Felice had no idea that the woman was a switch-hitter, much less a lesbian. But she had nonetheless introduced Felice into the pleasures of lesbian sex.

Felice was really confused then. She had no idea if she was truly a lesbian or not; yet she couldn't forget the ecstasy she had experienced in the woman's arms — her gentleness, her delicate explorings, her hot tongue. Initially, she'd tried to blame the woman for introducing her to lesbianism; but she couldn't. Without her own consent, it could never have happened at all. No, Felice had been ready to try anything. She was bored with Doug. There had to be more to married life than what they had. She wasn't sure of what . . . but something.

She wondered if letting a woman make love to her

constituted adultery. Felice supposed it did. Although there was nothing in the rulebook about having an affair with a member of one's own sex, still she had promised herself to Doug. Giving her body to someone else, of any gender, could only be considered a betrayal of her vows.

To the consternation of her Catholic parents, Felice filed for divorce. In the eyes of the church, she would always be considered Doug's wife; but in the eyes of the law, she was single again. Doug had been upset, yet relieved as well. It was as if he too had come to realize that they had married at too young an age. As for her Catholicism, Felice had never been all that involved with her religion. It was something she took for granted, like being a brunette or female. In times of great stress, she would pray; otherwise, she never thought about it. Felice believed in God and the Ten Commandments, but all the rest seemed to her to be nothing more than details, a lot of cluttering mumbo-jumbo – Felice preferred the direct approach to God.

She'd moved to New York City, gotten a job as a switchboard operator until she learned her way around town, and then had begun to take night classes at New York City College. She received her B.A. six years later, and went to work at Kloberg Publishing. In the interim, Felice had discovered gay bars. And women. And that she was most definitely, no-question-about-it, a lesbian. Young, extremely attractive, and naive – women found her exceptionally desirable. Most of them frightened her; they were too intense, too predatory, with a kind of desperation about them.

About two years after moving to Manhattan, Felice met Alegra Morris, a five-foot dervish of excess energy and madcap sexual appetites; pretty, intelligent, with a zany sense of humor, and an attitude toward life that made it all seem a game. Felice fell in love. She also learned things about sex she had never dreamed possible. However, Alegra was not one to stay tied to one person for any length of time. Even after they broke up, though, they remained friends and to the present day, Felice still considered Alegra to be a Lesbian Institution; a human source of learning that all lesbians should be exposed to.

Since then, Felice had had a few affairs with women; but nothing all that serious. She continued to take occasional courses in various subjects – Spanish, beginning piano, sailing – yet it disturbed her that she had no one to come home to; no one to share her life with. At thirty-four, Felice was beginning to feel time slipping away from her; not that she was getting old so much as a sense of her life having no meaning. And perhaps that had been the strongest underlying motivation for going on this cruise. Who she might meet, what might happen, she hadn't known; but at least it was a change, and an act of affirmative action.

". . . Isn't it a lovely party?"

Felice jumped at the unexpected interruption of her thinking, then recognized Margaret Anderson. "Oh, hi," she said, embarrassed. "I was a million miles away."

"She sure has been," Donna put in, taking another glass of champagne from the tray the waitress was carrying.

Sandy lifted a glass for herself, then obviously having second thoughts, handed it over to Felice. "I get silly with champagne."

"Everyone does . . . that's the point," Carmen remarked. "How are you enjoying the cruise so far, Margaret?" she asked the perfectly coiffed white-haired woman.

"It's been interesting," she replied cryptically.

Turning slightly, Felice put her glass down on the round table. "Would you like to dance?" she asked, almost shyly.

Margaret's smile was radiant. "Do you want to lead, or shall I?"

Felice laughed. "Are you a good lead?"

"Not very."

"Then I shall." As they sauntered toward the circular dance floor, Felice was suddenly aware of the amount of champagne she had already consumed. She felt wonderful. Alive. The huge Mazatlán Ballroom was a cacophony of women's voices, laughter, and inebriated Christmas merriment. As she took Margaret into her arms, Felice suddenly knew that they would end up in bed together that night. And apparently, Margaret sensed it too. Her eyes grew wide at Felice's touch, as if it presaged what would happen later in the evening. Laughing quietly to herself, Felice led the older woman to the rumba the orchestra was playing. It was an old tune; the sort that usually was heard on Muzak in elevators.

"Why are you laughing?" Margaret asked.

"I was just wondering if you used food coloring."

"On my hair?"

"No," Felice said, shaking her head. "In your eyes. I've never seen such blue eyes in all my life!"

¤ ¤ ¤

Lynn Adler undressed slowly before Marsha O'Shea's open-mouthed stare. The flirtation and necking of a few days before had been fun, but now it was time to get down to business. Her sense of triumph, of knowing just how she was affecting Marsha, was heady. Yet, to be certain that her expression wasn't giving away her real thoughts, Lynn turned her back on Marsha – with feigned reserve. "D-do you want . . . to touch me?"

"Oh my God!" Marsha reached for her, hands hot on Lynn's cool, sculptured body.

"I-I've never done this before, Marsha," Lynn lied. "Please be gentle and patient."

By then, Marsha's mouth was traveling down Lynn's torso, nesting in the soft rise of her abdomen, her hands pulling Lynn toward the bunk bed. "I will," she whispered. Then, as if the information had just sunk in, Marsha glanced up. "You've never gone to bed with a woman?"

"Never," Lynn replied, blinking her green eyes innocently.

"Then you've not come out?"

"Out," Lynn repeated softly. "Out where?"

"Oh wow! You really want to go through with this? Why are you on this cruise?"

"B-because," Lynn said, a look of injured martyrdom on her face, "I want to find out if I'm a lesbian."

Marsha licked her lips, her eyes roving over Lynn's body hungrily. "Well then, that's what we'll do. You sure you don't mind about my mastectomy?"

Lynn smiled like a saint. "Oh no! I think you're so wonderful, Marsha! Brave, too. Here let me touch you, kiss your scar. . . ."

¤ ¤ ¤

Carmen was enjoying a slight buzz from the champagne, but had judiciously refrained from overindulging. And now, taking a short stroll on the Promenade Deck to clear her head, she could see couples huddled, heads together, or holding hands and staring out to sea. The music from the ballroom below wafted up with the balmy breeze. Tomorrow they would put in at Mazatlân for two days, and she only hoped that all the passengers would find their way back to the ship at night; at least, the last night.

Suddenly Carmen thought she heard angry voices; worse, a man's voice. Hurrying toward the sounds, she rounded the corner in time to see one of the crew holding off one woman while he tried to kiss a resisting younger woman, his muscular arm holding her tightly against him.

"You goddam sonuvabitch," the woman at bay

screamed, "let go of her! She's not interested in you!"

"Aw, shut up! You damned dykes are all alike. Think you can fuck just like a man – and you can't. You can't even protect this pretty little cunt of yours much less fuck her!"

The older woman swung her leg back for a good kick at him when Carmen intervened. "What's your name, sailor," she demanded.

"What's it to you?"

He was visibly drunk, weaving, and his eyes were glazed and half closed. "I'm putting you on report. You may as well cooperate with me . . . there aren't all that many men aboard."

"Fuck off," he growled, though he let go of his captive. "You broads are all alike. Think you're so big and mighty. You can't even spare a guy a little kiss – "

"Your name," Carmen demanded again, furious.

"Nick. Second mate. What's yours, honey?" He began to lurch toward her.

"I'm the cruise coordinator, and you're on report. Get back to your quarters, sailor. The captain will want to see you in the morning."

"Captain's a damned asshole."

"I'm sure he'll be glad to learn that." She watched him as he lumbered away, stumbling from railing to the side of the Neptune Lounge. "I'm terribly sorry this happened," she told the two women.

"Men," the older one spat out. "What makes them think they can get away with that kind of stuff?"

"Because they are successful so often," Carmen replied calmly, trying to soothe her.

"I think I'll learn karate," the younger one said plaintively. "I was really scared."

"What'll you do to him?" the other inquired, her hands still balled into fists.

"That's up to the captain," Carmen answered. "Now,

why don't you two try to put this unfortunate incident out of your minds . . . go ahead and enjoy the rest of the evening." However, in her heart, Carmen knew that Captain Margolies would probably go easy on Nick. Though the captain was too well schooled to ever pull such a stunt with a woman, still she knew his sympathy would side with the second mate.

"I could use a drink," the mauled victim declared.

"Good idea," Carmen concurred. "I'll put it on my tab, okay?" *Well,* she thought, *another disaster narrowly averted.* It wasn't the first time some member of a crew had put the make on a passenger but on a lesbian cruise, it was untenable. Yet, to be totally fair, sometimes passengers encouraged it – perhaps even lesbian ones. A little too much to drink, curiosity, or just trying to make a lover jealous . . . where there were people, there were sex games. It seemed inevitable.

CHAPTER SEVEN

THE WEATHER HAD CHANGED from bright morning glare to an afternoon of sullen gray. The shrieks of pool-side fun had become mere echoes, and the chlorine-tinted water lapped at the sides of its confines; alone, useless and ignored as the first drops of rain began to fall upon the deck.

Staring at the abandoned pool, Felice was the only person still to be seen in the area; nursing a hangover plus a vodka and tonic. And it wasn't just the hangover that made her feel rotten, cheap, and weak; it was what she had done the night before. *How could I possibly have gone to bed with her?* she asked herself silently. But she knew the answer. She was lonely. And she had been hot as all hell.

THE CRUISE

A few drinks too many . . . the urgency in Margaret's light blue eyes . . . the need to share, to touch, to feel. . . .

She almost snorted in self-derision. Her friend Ann would call it a "mercy fuck" – but it wasn't true. Felice had needed Margaret with almost equal intensity. How long can a person go without feeling physically wanted, without sex? Yes, there was always masturbation, and Felice had indulged in her fair share of it. But masturbation was a deliberate act, a means of releasing the aching need without the sordidness of being a pickup in a bar. A two-edged deed. You could keep your dignity by playing with yourself . . . but you also had to acknowledge your carnal cravings and just how alone you really are.

Perhaps if Margaret hadn't been so apologetic, hadn't insisted on only a sliver of light from the bathroom . . . maybe it wouldn't have been such a bummer today.

"No, please, Felice," she had said as they entered Margaret's stateroom. "Don't turn on the lights."

"Just a lamp so I don't break a leg," Felice had replied, half teasing and half serious. She had never liked making love in the dark; it made it seem stealthy. Weaving slightly, well aware that she'd had entirely too much champagne to drink, she saw Margaret's blur step over to the bathroom and switch on the stark light . . .then close the door so only a crack showed through.

Margaret came back to her then, placing warm palms on either side of Felice's face. "I've been wanting to do this since that first night out, when I found you watching the stars. You're very lovely, my dear."

Her voice was husky, cracking slightly with her emotion; and Margaret leaned forward, placing her lips on Felice's, softly, gently.

But for Felice, the contact ignited long suppressed feelings and she ran her nails up Margaret's bare arms, then pulled the older woman closer. She wanted to feel a woman's breasts against hers, feel the heat and softness; she wanted to rub her pelvis against Margaret's, grind the intensity of her many lonely years into oblivion. But Felice didn't think that Margaret would understand that; it would probably only frighten her. Instead, Felice began to take the hairpins from Margaret's French twist, letting them drop to the carpeted floor soundlessly, as the woman's white hair fell to her shoulders.

Their lips melded with restrained ardor, sliding across in moist pliancy, testing. Slowly, Felice's tongue came forward as her lips parted more, and she was elated when Margaret offered no resistance. In fact, quite the reverse. The older woman groaned deep in her throat as their tongues writhed in hot searching. Arching her back, thrusting her full breasts against Felice's, the woman eased them both toward the bed without breaking the kiss.

Felice felt the inside of her thighs grow taut with anticipation, and her clitoris began to throb in awakening. It had been so long, so goddamn long since she'd been made love to!

Margaret's hands began to unfasten the hook of Felice's bra from beneath the pale blue tunic top she was wearing, and then her small hands fluttered across Felice's breasts as if she didn't dare be too aggressive. Moaning again, the woman lifted the top just enough to reveal Felice's creamy breasts, and she lowered her face to nuzzle against them, pushing the globes against her face as if to suffocate herself.

Breathing quickly by then, Felice had pulled the tunic off and then slipped out of her bra. In the shaft of light, she could clearly see the demarcation of her tan where the bathing suit began to protect the ivory complexion of her breasts. Half-lidded eyes watched Margaret take an aroused nipple into her mouth, tonguing it gently as her hand kneaded the other breast.

"Take off your clothes," Felice whispered hungrily. "I want to feel you against me. Hurry, Margaret . . . I need you, and I need you now!"

Shyly, she turned her back to Felice and took her clothes off quickly, tossing them onto a chair. "I-I'm no youngster, darling," she had said slowly.

Felice had noticed the four-hooked bra and didn't expect the woman to have the muscle tone of a twenty-year-old. The skin on the underside of her arms had begun to wrinkle, though not offensively so, and there was a deep arc of flesh from her waist up her back. She saw it, and she didn't care. It was the contact with another human being she craved so desperately, the feeling of being wanted . . . loved . . . touched everywhere. "Come here," she said gently. "Let me kiss you again."

"I'm old enough to be your mother," Margaret said, her voice breaking.

Felice raised up on one elbow, letting her free hand reach around to fondle Margaret's breast as she kissed the woman's back. By then Felice was too hot to think about such things as differences in age. She wanted to throw her legs wide apart, to give as much pleasure to this woman as she hoped to receive. But she was also sensitive to Margaret's feelings, her fear of rejection because she no longer had a firm, supple body. "I think you're lovely, Margaret. I didn't come here with you because I expected a young movie star . . . but because of *who* you are. Not all young women have beautiful bodies, so you shouldn't be ashamed of what age has done to yours," she soothed. "Doesn't a kiss taste just as sweet now as it did twenty years ago?"

Margaret laughed briefly. "Far sweeter."

"Does my touching you . . . here; or kissing you . . . there . . . feel as good?"

"Better than you could possibly know," Margaret said, already beginning to turn around to face her, to lower herself against Felice.

"And my arms about your neck, my hands caressing your buttocks?"

THE CRUISE

"My God, Felice, my God!"

Their legs had intertwined as they kissed deeply, sucking on one another as if for sustenance. The sensations as their nipples grazed, warm flesh sinking onto warm flesh, the delicious suspense of woman loving woman – not quickly, not harshly, but slowly, savoring every moment – had Felice ready to burst with pent up excitement. She had felt herself begin to perspire, her body aching to press closer and closer, the cheeks of her buttocks tensing in a pleading dance for more and more. . . .

No, Felice thought now, recalling last night, it had been the wrong thing to do. No matter how she rationalized it today, she should never have gone with Margaret. Afterward, the woman had wept, clinging to Felice, mouthing how much she loved her against her throat. It was a stupid mistake, Felice realized, staring at the abandoned swimming pool. Now Margaret would follow her everywhere for the rest of the cruise with an injured look in her lovely blue eyes. *How can I tell her that it was only that once, a coming together out of common need – but not love.* Last night had been sex, and that was all. A younger woman would understand that right away; not have taken their hours together so personally. But at Margaret's age? What had she said? Oh yes. "Nobody loves you when you're old and gay."

How would she extricate herself from Margaret's gratitude? Was there anything in the world that could make a person feel more guilty than misguided gratitude?

"Hello there! Merry Christmas!"

Felice winced as she recognized Margaret's voice, but she managed to turn around and smile. "Hi. Hope you're feeling better than I am."

Margaret was wearing a one-piece bathing suit, with a towel about her shoulders. Her large blue eyes were clear and filled with something akin to merriment. "I feel great," she said as she sat down opposite Felice at the umbrella table. "Do 'we' have a bit of a hangover today?"

"Ohh, yes indeed we do," she answered, a somewhat perplexed expression in her brown eyes. "You're not going for a swim in the rain, are you?"

"Why not? It doesn't make you any wetter," she responded with a broad smile. "Why don't you join me? It would make you feel better."

"You're incredible," Felice said, not quite knowing what to make of Margaret's detached good humor.

"No, not really. But you did me a very big favor last night, Felice. One you won't fully understand until you've reached my age."

"I. . . ."

"No, let me finish. I know I said a lot of things that are probably worrying you today, but forget about them. It isn't that I didn't mean them at the time, only that they weren't really true." She glanced down at the table top and her manicured nails played with a bump in the paint. "I've spent the past ten years feeling older and older, uglier and uglier . . . I've wasted ten whole years fearing rejection. I loved you last night because you made me realize that I'm not dead, not over the hill . . . that I can still find someone who will love me just as I am. Wrinkles, sags, and all . . . none of it matters. Not any more."

Felice could only stare at her, not knowing what to say or think. "Well, I. . . ."

Margaret held up her hand, a tender expression on her face. "Somewhere, Felice, there is a woman in my age bracket who will love me. She might be five years younger than I am, or older – but we'll both know, and accept, that youth is physical beauty only. A kiss, as you asked last night, is infinitely sweeter when you have the maturity to appreciate its meaning. When you're young, sex is urgent . . . almost a necessity for one's self-image. Later . . . now, that is, it's sharing, giving of one's self. And perhaps more importantly, accepting the love of your partner."

A slow smile crossed Felice's oval face. She didn't

know precisely what Margaret was talking about and she accepted that. She had not reached an age to worry about rejection on the sole basis of her physical body tone. But she listened to Margaret, saw the intensity in the woman's eyes, and thought she could understand what it might be like. "You're quite a remarkable woman, Margaret Anderson."

Her mouth curled into a mischievous smile. "Yes, and thanks to you, I now realize it. There's plenty of life in this old frame and I intend to live every moment of it!" She broke into a laugh, almost a bubbling release. "Now, are you going to take that swim with me, or not?"

Felice stood up, then leaned over and kissed Margaret on the forehead. "Not I. *This* old frame is going to get another drink! I have to get my blood back up to eighty proof or I'll die!"

"Ahh, it's true, it's true. Youth is wasted on the young!"

"See you later?" Felice inquired as she straightened up.

"If you're planning to go to the Fish Net Disco, maybe. But this cruise won't last forever, and I intend to make the most of it. I've been giving some thought to Lynn Adler. She seems more than mildly anxious to have a good time."

"Really? I had more the impression that she was terribly aloof . . . but I'm with you, tiger," Felice replied, laughing.

"See you," Margaret said, then draped her towel over the arm of the chair and walked to the edge of the pool.

Felice watched her as she expertly dove in. "Mercy fuck my ass," she muttered under her breath, smiling. *And a Merry Christmas to you too, Margaret*, she thought.

¤ ¤ ¤

Alone, Erika strolled toward the bar on the Promenade Deck hoping Bernie would be on duty. Fortunately, Charlene had made inroads with one of the women they'd met that evening after the layover in Ensenada. Her name was Sue or Susan – something like that – and Erika had found her terribly dull. The snobbish type from the academic world with a Ph.D. in ecomonics or political science or one of those . . . and apparently quite "important" in the Women's Movement. Whatever that meant. However, she was the sort of person whom Charlene would, naturally, find fascinating. A product of Radcliffe, and then on to Princeton for her postgraduate work. Charlene's excuse to ingratiate herself was all too obvious: Perhaps Sue would like to write a book, which Charlene could agent. . .?

In just four days, Erika had had enough exposure to the woman to decide that even if she wrote twenty books, only another Ph.D. might understand what she had to say – if anything – and at that, Erika was certain that readers would be lying about their comprehension. If there was anything Erika couldn't stand it was overeducated phonies turning each other on with a lot of incomprehensible gibberish. Even the woman's business card had been a turn-off: *Dr. Sue* whatever her last name was. It implied that the woman was a physician; while it was proper to address a Ph.D. as "doctor," putting it on her business card was, to Erika, just so much screwing around. Of all the scholars she had met over the years – and there had been quite a few – only those who dispensed with appending their degrees had been of any interest to her. They were down to earth, casual, and unless it came up in conversation covering a specific area of expertise, Erika would never have known they'd even gone to college much less held higher degrees. *Those* people she liked. The ones like Sue were just pains in the ass, with fingers in each ear so they couldn't hear anyone else speaking except themselves.

Opening the door to the Neptune Lounge, her face

broke into a warm, open smile at the sight of Bernie. She glanced about and was surprised to see that the room was fairly crowded despite so early an hour in the afternoon. It was, after all, Christmas Day. Perhaps, she thought, as in her own case, these people just didn't take the holiday as particularly religious. Even though Erika had been raised as a Methodist, by the time she was in her late teens, she'd abandoned the religion. None of Christianity made any sense to her . . . and she'd long since learned that there wasn't anything in the Christian faith that hadn't been said by Far East religions centuries before the birth of Christ.

In fact, beginning with the Old Testament, Erika had had a hard time believing the Bible. She could still recall getting into an argument with her mother over it. "If it's in the Bible, it's true," her mother had told her one day.

Tall and gangly at eighteen, Erika had risked contradicting her. "How can you say that?"

"Why shouldn't I?" her mother had asked, a look of shocked dismay on her prematurely lined face.

Erika had slouched on the kitchen chair and taken a deep breath.

"Answer me," her mother demanded, her color rising.

"Mom," she'd begun hesitantly. "Let's just take the Garden of Eden."

"Go on," her mother urged with tight-lipped disapproval.

"There's only Adam and Eve, right? And they have two kids, Cain and Abel, right?"

"Go on."

Swallowing, Erika had proceeded. "Just four people on the face of the earth. Cain kills Abel, so that leaves three."

"So?"

She'd looked at her mother with large, clear gray eyes. "God's punishment, mom, was to banish Cain to a village, where he married and raised kids of his own.

Where'd the other village come from?"

Her mother had stared at her for what seemed an eternity. "That's blasphemy," she had retorted in a menacingly low voice.

"You're not explaining where the other people came from."

"Nor do I intend to," she'd retorted with obvious control. "It's in the good book, and that's all you have to know. The Bible says it happened, and that means it did."

Things at home never did get back to normal after that exchange. It was as if Mrs. Schultz had decided she'd given birth to a freak, an unavoidable embarrassment in teenage form that she couldn't quite throw out onto the street . . . but would prefer to pretend didn't exist. Erika wasn't stupid. She'd caught on very quickly, and began making her plans to leave home. There wasn't really all that much to "leave" anyway. Her dad had died three years before, another victim to the foul air of the coal mines of Pennsylvania. She had no siblings, and now her mother had shut her out. There were no opportunities in her hometown . . . except for mining, and they didn't permit women.

She couldn't type or take shorthand, and the only job she'd been able to find since leaving high school was as a waitress in a seedy saloon that catered to the grime-streaked miners and a few sleezy married men taking their bimbos to a place where their wives wouldn't think to look for them.

And Erika had known that she would never be happy getting married and spending the rest of her life in that town. Guys were okay, but she expected better than what she saw around her. There were cities to be seen, continents to be explored. She didn't know where she'd go, or how she'd end up, but Erika knew she couldn't possibly stay where she was. And too, Erika wanted to find out who she really was. Though she dated occasionally, she had found herself deeply disturbed and attracted by some of her female classmates. She didn't know precisely what that indicated, but Erika doubted that it was "normal." When these classmates *ooh*ed and *ahh*ed over one of the guys in school, Erika could've thrown up. They were just jocks without a brain in their heads – all brawn, looking to score – who'd one day end up in the mines. No future. No, there had to be more. Somewhere.

Erika hitchhiked to New York City and swiftly discovered that it was no place for anyone down and out. Sure, it held a lot of promise to newcomers . . . but it only glittered for those who had already made their way to the top. She landed a job at Sardi's as a hatcheck girl; then she met Artie, a "lieutenant" in the Mafia. She'd begun to fill out by then, unaware that she was a striking young woman – not beautiful in the usual sense, but a head-turner. And Artie became her tutor. He bought her fashionable clothes, showed her how to walk, hold her head, use her hands. She didn't especially enjoy going to bed with Artie; but she didn't particularly mind it, either.

What she liked, though, was living in his Park Avenue apartment; having the doorman tip his hat to her whenever she passed by. Through Artie, she was learning how the other half lived – and she loved it. Then Artie got her a job as a photographer's model, and Erika began to realize just how very attractive men found her. She'd been suspicious at first, telling Artie: "I'm too tall, too leggy, and my face is too thin."

"Forget it," he'd told her. "What you've got, baby, ain't found any too many times. You've got the look of class, see. And a sort of way about you that says 'Keep your mitts off.' Like, maybe, you was a wild animal, like a cat that can't be tamed. Ain't many guys that can resist that kind of dare."

Erika had given Artie's reply a great deal of thought. If he was right, then she was being stupid not to take advantage of it. Maybe she shouldn't be a model after all; it was boring, and though it paid pretty well, what would she do when she got older? One wrinkle and it was all over until she became old enough to beg for work in Geritol ads.

About three months later, with almost five thousand bucks in the bank, Erika kissed off Artie. When she'd said she was leaving, he'd beaten her up, told her to stay out of his sight or risk a worse beating; but that didn't frighten her. She'd fought back and Artie hadn't looked too wonderful either.

However, discretion always the better part of valor, Erika went to Spain. At that time, her five thousand dollars was like ten times that much in a country where you could loll on the beach all day long and have a superb dinner for roughly twenty-five cents. Booze was contraband and dirt cheap, and she was having the time of her life. In the evenings, she could nurse a scotch and water at any cafe and watch the flamenco dancers; or on Sundays, join in with the local *sardanas* . . . which she later learned was introduced to the country in its early history when there was so much trade with the ancient Greeks. The steps to the dance were practically identical.

Her tall blonde good looks and ready-to-laugh gray eyes made her very popular with everyone, and she'd learned enough Spanish to get around; which pleased the locals since it showed that she respected their language and ways. The following summer, Erika met Bianca Genovese – the wife of a business tycoon from Chicago. On a how-do-you-do, Erika knew she was in love. Not a crush, not just uncomfortable – but wildly, madly in love. And Bianca returned the feeling wholeheartedly. With her husband still in Chicago, not even planning to join Bianca during her holiday, the two women spent more time in bed than out of it.

If there was any gossip, neither of them heard it.

However, as Erika pointed out one lazy afternoon, stretched out stark naked, smoking a cigarette: "The Spanish aren't much for gossiping beyond neighborhood squabbles. I figure they think all foreigners are kind of strange in the first place . . . so why waste time wondering what they're up to?"

Then, when it was time for Bianca to return to Chicago, she convinced Erika to go with her. "What about your husband?" Erika had asked.

"What about him?"

Erika had grinned. "Cross that bridge when we come to it?"

"Exactly. Besides, he's got plenty of connections. If I ask him nicely, he'll find you something to do."

"And what if he finds out about . . . us?"

"Don't worry, he won't."

But he did, of course. Suspecting Bianca of infidelity when she no longer spent as much time at home as she had before her vacation, he'd put a detective on her trail. Four months after their return to Chicago, her husband had somehow obtained a passkey from the building manager, and simply let himself into Erika's apartment on the North Shore as the two women were writhing in sexual ecstasy. "Now, isn't this a cozy picture?" he'd asked, leaning against the bedroom doorway.

Bianca had burst into tears while Erika hastily threw on a robe. She'd expected him to be furious, to scream or even beat her up, but he didn't. Instead, he began to undress. "Can three play this game?" he'd asked, just as politely as if he'd found them sipping tea and decided to join them.

A few days later, he telephoned Erika and made her an offer. "A friend of mine wants to open up a queer joint and needs somebody to front it."

"Are you kidding? If the place gets busted, I'll go to prison."

"If you don't, I'll file for a divorce and name you as corespondent. It's against the law to be a dyke, Erika. For myself, I don't care much. I'm happier knowing that Bianca goes for women instead of other men. I'd kill her if I ever found her with a man."

"Then why are you blackmailing me into this deal?"

"As I said, it's a favor for a friend. Besides, I'm a major stockholder, so to speak. We want a really nice place where dykes and their fems can have an enjoyable evening out – a nice restaurant with good food, good booze, no problem with the fuzz. Maybe even a small band for dancing."

Erika had scarcely been able to believe her ears. "What makes you so confident the law won't raid the place?"

He'd laughed. "This is Chicago, Erika. Money will buy you anything in this town."

"This isn't a Syndicate operation, is it?" she'd asked, thinking about Artie's threats.

"What do you care? Look, Erika, you don't seem to understand your position very well. You're a pervert in the eyes of society and the law. You've been bedding my wife and God knows who else's –"

"Hey! Back off . . . I'd never been to bed with any woman till Bianca."

His chuckle was mean and low. "It's funny how such a pretty name sounds dirty coming from you."

Erika had been too shocked to retort.

"What you are, Erika," he'd continued, "is no better or worse than the Syndicate. You want to live your own way and be left alone; so do they."

"I'm no killer," she'd finally managed to say.

"No? Morally, you are. At least, most people's morality. Take it or leave it, Erika. Fronting the place could make you very, very rich. The alternative is to have your name dragged through the courts, make headline news, create a situation where neither you nor Bianca will ever be able to live in peace –"

She was in no position to try to point out to him that comparing lesbianism to murder made about as much sense as saying heterosexuals created wars – though that was probably closer to the truth than what he was suggesting.

"Okay, okay," she'd replied. "I get the picture."

"I thought you would."

And that had been the start of her "career." Once she had had a little time to think about her situation, she began to enjoy her work. She had had to learn everything about the business from scratch: supervising the chef and waitresses; making sure she got the best prices for food and liquor; seeing to it that everything ran smoothly and efficiently; finding a butch bruiser for a bouncer; learning the ropes about screening customers before they were permitted to enter – if they didn't say "Dorothy sent me," they couldn't enter – and all the countless details of overseeing a restaurant.

If the real owners were Mafioso, no one ever spoke of it. In fact, Erika had never met such nice, caring people. They treated her with total respect, and if she needed anything, they were quick to see to it that she got it. And she didn't have to worry about Artie, either. These men would protect her. For all she knew, he may have already been told to lay off.

Because of the grueling hours, she saw less and less of Bianca – who was, unfortunately, becoming a drag with jealous scenes. Erika's ardor waned, and soon thereafter, Bianca's husband sent his wife on a tour of the Greek Isles. Not too much later, Erika learned that Bianca had taken up with a famous Greek actress. In a way, she was saddened by the information; Bianca had been her "first love"; on the other hand, it was also a relief. Erika wanted fun and laughs and a good time in bed, not a nag at the other end of a tugging leash. Commitments and vows were for straight people, the ones with the mortgages and similar stifling burdens. That wasn't for her. This was her youth, the best years of her life; and she was making more money than she'd ever dreamed anyone could. Why should she saddle herself with all the same traps that heterosexuals had to endure? And later, of course, she'd moved on to the New York scene.

". . . Hello, Rick."

Erika brought herself out of Memory Lane like a deer hearing a twig snap. Glancing to her right, she smiled broadly as she gazed into the vivid green eyes of Lynn Adler. "Why, hello, Legs," she answered, swiftly taking in the smooth creamy flesh exposed by the low-cut dress.

Lynn looked up at her through thick, dark lashes, a little shy and reserved. "Isn't your . . . friend with you?"

She shook her head slowly. "Charlene Coldspot is otherwise engaged," Erika said with a low laugh.

"Then . . . may I buy you a drink?"

"Legs, you can do anything you like with me."

Lynn's lips parted knowingly. "Anything?"

"Would I lie to you?"

Linking her arm through Erika's, Lynn pressed her breast against Erika. "I'll have to test you before this voyage is over."

"You couldn't ask for a more willing subject."

"Speaking of, how's your book coming along?"

"Who cares?" Erika replied, suddenly feeling young and carefree . . . ready to laugh or make love – whichever came first.

CHAPTER EIGHT

UNCONVENTIONAL RELIGIOUS SERVICES had been conducted earlier in the day by women active in their respective faiths . . . inclusive of a special service to pay homage to Goddess. Donna and Sandy had attended the Protestant worship, which had been led by the ship's physician, Amanda Holden. It had been a deeply moving experience for Donna in particular.

Dr. Holden had held her enthralled by her quiet strength and obvious devotion. A woman of unusual dignity, she spoke to them of Mary Magdalen and Christ's invitation to the assembled that those without sin throw the first stone. Dr. Holden explored the deeper message, sharing her convictions in a reserved yet conversational manner. "I've thought about that passage more times than I can recount," she had said, a self-deprecating smile on her lips. "There were no jobs for women in Biblical times . . . no factories, no coffee shops. If a woman was of marriageable age, yet had no husband . . . how was she supposed to support herself? Jesus recognized her predicament and did *not* 'forgive' her, because He saw nothing to forgive. She was surviving the only way she knew how; the way society had structured life, she had no choice. And I believe that Jesus knew that, accepted it."

Amanda looked about the large room that had been set up for the service, her dark eyes somber. "And I believe He accepts our lesbianism for the same reasons. I don't believe that He looks at us as 'sinners,' in need of forgiveness or conversion. He sees us for what we really are: God-fearing human beings, living our lives the only way *we* know how. Wouldn't it be a far greater sin to marry a man without love, to give our bodies to men only because that's what most women do? Would we not be making prostitutes of ourselves simply to appease society's expectations? There's more to marriage than cooking, laundry, and producing babies. There's a moral responsibility to care deeply about the person you marry, to share the ups and the downs . . . could any of us do that with a man?"

There had been a general murmuring of agreement that such would be out of the question, and Amanda resumed. "To live such a life would be a *lie*. How can we serve God if we live with deceit in our hearts? The only way any of us in this room can be whole is to be honest with ourselves. If there's sin in that, I can't find it. We aren't accepting a man's protection, or his emotional or financial support, on false pretenses . . . isn't that, in the long run, far more Christian? If there was anything Jesus despised, it was hypocrisy. No one here said, at the age of three or five or even fifteen: 'I think I'll be a lesbian when

I grow up.' No. It was something each of us discovered about ourselves along the way. To be a lesbian, even in today's more open atmosphere, is to risk having a lot of stones thrown at you. Yet we do it. Why? Because we accept ourselves, and in so doing, free our minds and souls from guilt and self-hate that would infringe upon the love that we should be giving to Jesus. On this day, a child was born to Mary and Joseph. A child who influenced history as perhaps no other human ever has. Jesus preached love, compassion, and tolerance . . . I cannot believe He meant to exclude lesbians."

The sermon had gone on for another ten or fifteen minutes, and had ended with a hearty chorus of "Amazing Grace" sung by all. But later, Donna had had much to reflect on. She'd never heard a woman preacher before, and somehow, the words that were directed so unequivocally to lesbians conveyed a deeper, greater impact. Donna had always sort of thought that when Judgment Day came, she'd somehow muddle through – perhaps unnoticed, or something. But Dr. Holden had made her see that Jesus was a compassionate man, not one to punish her for being something she couldn't help. Like having two arms and one head, her lesbiansim was a part of her; as fundamental as hunger, sleep, and the need to protect herself from the elements. As Dr. Holden had said, if God hadn't wanted homosexuality to exist . . . it wouldn't – even as humans had no wings to fly with. "We're all God's creatures, more given to helping others than inflicting any harm. If it's 'unnatural' to be a lesbian, it's equally 'unnatural' to be celibate. Do any of you believe that the Gates of Heaven will be closed to nuns and monks?"

Over brunch, as the others at the table chatted, Donna had pondered that question. It *was* contrary to human nature to deny oneself any sexual outlet. That it was done on the premise that celibacy was a means of channeling all one's energies in the service of God didn't make it any less contrary to the laws of nature. And as for the alleged "laws of nature," what about those lesbian seagulls on Catalina Island, off the coast of California? Or the fact that homosexuality and lesbianism existed among cats, dogs, primates, and other creatures?

For years, Donna had maintained a large scrapbook with clippings of articles from newspapers and magazines that showed homosexuality to be quite within the order of things; or where gay men and women were written up favorably as brave, law-abiding, upstanding citizens of a community. When she and Sandy had first gotten together, Sandy had teased her about it quite a bit. However, once Donna had explained her purpose, Sandy had been quick to understand. "Right now," Donna had told her, "my folks have no idea that I'm gay. They think I'm too fussy about who I marry, but they don't suspect anything else. One day, though," she'd said, "they will get suspicious and ask me point-blank, or they'll hear that I'm a lesbian from some other source. This," she continued, tapping the scrapbook, "is my 'defense.' They'll be horrified to learn the truth, but these clippings might help them to accept that I'm not some kind of monster."

And too, since Sandy had only been twenty-six at the time, Donna had asked her to peruse the scrapbook for her own benefit. Sandy had never had a lesbian experience before, and if they were going to spend the rest of their lives together, Donna wanted her to take a measure of pride in just what she really was. She didn't want Sandy to feel inferior, or strange. Living with another person was hard enough when everything was working in the couple's favor – but if one of them resented what she was, what people whispered about, the relationship would be destroyed in no time. Donna had learned that the hard way; two of her best friends had broken up after fifteen years for just that reason. Once the novelty of a relationship was over, the consuming passion, and people had to live with the reality of lesbiansim, it could begin to eat away and corrupt the love they'd once shared. Donna never wanted that to happen to them.

And once Sandy and she had decided that they were good for each other, that they had common goals and dreams, Donna had proposed marriage. "There are preachers who'll perform the ceremony, hon, and we'll find one."

She couldn't help smiling to herself as she recalled Sandy's reaction. Her blue eyes had misted despite a broad smile. "Could we have a double-ring wedding?"

"Anything you want, hon, anything at all." And they'd been formally, if not legally, married a few months later. That had been ten years before, when Donna had only been thirty. She had been trying to make something of her life by going to college part-time studying law enforcement. She was proud to be an American, and she wanted to contribute whatever she could to be sure the Great Society would flourish. And the best way she could think to accomplish that was to involve herself with the prevention of crime. Her job at the insurance company was all right, as far as it went; but it didn't give Donna a sense of accomplishment, of being a part of the mainstream. Becoming a parole officer had changed her entire life, and she loved her work. It was grueling, sometimes heartbreaking, but it served a real purpose, gave her a reason to want to fight the traffic on the Hollywood Freeway.

She'd been commended several times, and stabbed once – in the arm, by a spaced-out kid who'd managed, somehow, to obtain the weapon. Donna had decked her, but otherwise held no animosity. It wasn't up to her to pass judgment on the unfortunates, deranged, or deprived of society; that she left to others . . . and to God. Sometimes it was very difficult to keep her detached outlook, but she tried as hard as she could.

THE CRUISE

"You're awfully quiet today, darling," Sandy said, placing a warm roll on Donna's plate. "Don't you feel well?"

"Me? No, I'm fine, hon, just thinking." She glanced about to see if any of the others had noted her silence, wondering where Mac and Carol had gone off to . . . they never missed a meal. "What did you think about the sermon today?"

Sandy's round face became momentarily serious. "I don't know," she began slowly, passing the marmalade to Donna. "Kind of strange, I guess. I mean, it felt sort of funny to have a woman leading the service, and then, on Christmas Day, to be talking about Jesus loving us even though we're . . . lesbians." Her voice dropped with the last word as if she feared someone would overhear.

Donna laughed. "Why are you whispering?"

Sandy smiled and shrugged. "Habit, I guess." She took a bite of her Eggs Benedict and pursed her lips with appreciation. "I wish I could make them like this," she said almost to herself. "What about you? What'd you think of the service?"

Donna leaned back on her chair, her weathered face pensive. "I thought it was downright inspiring, that's what. Think about it, hon. Some day, there'll be churches and synagogues that welcome us all equally. Wouldn't that be something?" She tilted her chair back on its rear legs. "Wouldn't it be great to know that we could just be ourselves, living our lives like we always do but without fear of censure?"

"It'll never happen," Olga interrupted from the other side of the table.

"Why not?" Donna asked, genuinely interested in the woman's response.

"Because society has always needed a scapegoat and always will. Whether sneering at slaves in Ancient Rome, or at the blacks and the Jews, the Mexicans and Puerto

Ricans . . . society has to have a whipping post. It's not chic anymore to make fun of minorities because of their national origins or color . . . so now it's the queers and lesbians."

"Always was, wasn't it?" Sandy inquired, buttering her roll.

"It's more concentrated now, better organized, too. Look at the Moral Majority."

"Wait a sec, what about the National Gay Task Force?" Donna put in.

"And the civil liberties groups," Pinky added, a reproachful tone in her gravely voice.

Olga lifted her ample shoulders in dismissal. "Who controls the big money? Who's got television networks scared silly to say anything honest . . . and who's telling senate committees how to word obscenity bills? The Moral Majority."

Sandy sipped from her Bloody Mary thoughtfully. "Well, I've got to admit I don't approve of obsenity."

Olga smiled patiently. "Can you define it? Even the Supreme Court begs off trying to say just what is obscene and what isn't. Do you know that those self-righteous idiots would be thrilled if they could put *Ms.* magazine out of business?"

Sandy leaned forward. "But why? It's not obscene!"

"They think it is. Not because of pornographic content so much as because they fear that feminists are undermining the family nucleus."

"That's stupid," Sandy declared emphatically. "Feminists have husbands and babies too."

"Be that as it may," Olga replied, "the Jerry Falwells of this country want to put every woman back in the oven – where she belongs, according the them."

"In the oven!" Sandy blurted, shocked.

"Just a figure of speech, hon," Donna quickly soothed. "Like keeping us barefoot and pregnant."

"Exactly," Olga concurred, finishing her scrambled eggs with a flourish. "If it were up to them, we wouldn't have the vote anymore."

"Shee-it," Barbara interrupted, thrusting a cigarette into her mouth as she pushed away her plate. "It's all a bunch of crap. None of them guys can do much. They ain't no majority an' all of us knows it."

Olga's expression was one of controlled pity. "That's what the Jews said when Hitler was coming into power . . . and even later."

Just then, Carmen Navasky strode into the dining room, smiling and waving to a number of the passengers as she made her way toward Donna's table.

"Here comes Doris Day," Pinky warned softly with a meaningful glance over Donna's shoulder.

"I saw her in the mirror," Donna responded. "And she's not a bad sort, Pinky. Just doing her job. . . ."

The short, thin woman shrugged. "I can't never get used to lesbians who try to pass . . . don't trust 'em."

Donna grinned. "Olga could pass – so could Sandy or even Carol."

"That's different," Pinky countered. "They're fems, that's all. But they live with *us*, taking good care of us and our homes."

Olga smiled. "You're suffering from reverse prejudice, Pinky."

The woman slapped her hand into the air. "Don't give me none of that fancy talk, Olga."

She leaned over and pecked Pinky on the cheek affectionately. "If you don't like being discriminated against, wouldn't it be wiser not to discriminate against others?"

"Why're you always gettin' on my case, Olga?"

Donna shook her head and winked at Sandy. In their brief acquaintance, she had yet to be able to figure out what Olga saw in wiry Pinky. Where Olga was intelligent and educated, a professional person, Pinky was the total opposite. Donna strongly doubted that even a fantastic sex life would be enough to hold them together. Yet, despite Pinky's whining ways, each of them seemed quite happy with the relationship. Donna didn't understand it; but then, it wasn't any of her business anyhow.

"Could you spare me a minute, Donna?" Carmen asked, a permission-seeking smile aimed at Sandy.

"Sure," Donna answered, getting to her feet. In the background, she heard the P.A. system broadcasting Christmas carols and briefly wondered how Mutt and Bojangles were doing at the kennel. She followed Carmen Navasky just outside the dining room aft of Deck 6, and as the sun glinted off Carmen's dark brown hair, Donna was keenly aware of how different they were from each other. Perfectly groomed, her deep tan showing off her real gold jewelry, Donna felt like a kid about to be reprimanded by the teacher. There was an aura of authority about the cruise coordinator, a manner that conveyed assurance and poise. She didn't know why super-feminine women made her feel that way – they just did. Donna was so ill at ease that she didn't know how to act or what to do.

"I hate to have to bring this up," Carmen began, a regretful expression in her velvety brown eyes, "but I have no choice."

"What's up?" Donna tried to hide her discomfort but doubted that she was succeeding.

Carmen gazed out to the horizon as if organizing her thoughts. "I've had a complaint, Donna. I want you to know, to accept, that I don't believe it for a second. But if I don't get your side of the story, the rest of this cruise could be very unpleasant for you."

Donna laughed self-consciously, not knowing what to expect next. "Am I using the wrong fork or something?"

Carmen shook her head slowly. "Gambling is perfectly legal aboard any liner once it's beyond the two-mile limit of the mainland."

Donna squinted at her. "What's gambling got to do . . . ?"

The other woman closed her eyes with a quick nod. "I'm getting to that, Donna. You see, one of the passengers came to me this morning and said you'd been winning at poker every day since we set sail . . . she accused you of cheating."

Stunned, Donna stared at her mutely for a second, then snorted. "Carol. That's who it was, wasn't it," she stated flatly.

Carmen's manicured hand went to Donna's arm. "I won't lie to you . . . you've a right to know."

"Was Mac with her, or was she all alone?"

"Her friend was with her, though I didn't get her name."

"About thirty-five, short haircut, hefty?"

"That fits," Carmen replied sympathetically.

"Didn't Mac say anything?"

"No. But I could tell she was terribly uncomfortable and would rather have been in a kyack going over Niagara Falls."

Donna looked down at her Western boots, noticing they needed a good spit-and-polish, wondering what she should say. To be accused of cheating at cards was no minor thing. And of course, now she understood why Mac and Carol hadn't been at their table this morning. How many other people had Carol told this to, she questioned. And what did it matter, she answered herself. Donna felt tears stinging her pale blue eyes but knew she could never permit herself to cry. Dammit, but it hurt. Why did people have to be so rotten? And she was very glad that Sandy wasn't present to hear about this – Sandy would claw Carol's eyes out if she knew the lies the woman had been telling.

Carmen cupped Donna's chin gently, lifting her face.

"It isn't true, is it?"

"No. Not a word of it. We're using the ship's decks of cards, and I haven't got X-ray vision. I'm just a much better poker player than Mac is."

"How much have you won so far?"

"From Mac alone?" Donna shrugged. "I don't know. We almost always have at least four players. Maybe four, five hundred – though I doubt that much." She smiled helplessly. "What do the others think? Do they say I've been cheating too?"

"I haven't asked them," Carmen answered. "I don't think it's necessary." She gazed at Donna sympathetically. "I've changed the dining room seating for those two so you won't have to be in the same room at the same time. However, there's nothing I can do if they want to be in the game lounge when you are."

"Thanks. I know there's just so much you can do."

Carmen frowned slightly. "Why do you think Carol made that accusation?" she asked simply.

Donna cocked her head to one side. "My impression, several days ago, was that Mac can't afford to lose. But I've never egged her into a game. She always insists, saying she's got to win back the money."

"So this could be nothing more than a means of keeping Mac in tow . . . or even a way to salve her ego while insuring Mac won't lose any more."

"I guess so. I couldn't say. I suppose I'd just better not play poker anymore."

Carmen's smile was beguiling. "Oh, I don't think that's necessary."

Donna glanced at her quizzically.

The younger woman looked deceptively innocent. "A few well-chosen and well-placed words should suffice to turn the rumor around. Shipboard gossip travels quickly," she added.

Grinning, Donna asked: "Do you think it'll work?"

"Do we have anything to lose?"
"No, ma'am – not a thing," Donna agreed readily.

¤ ¤ ¤

"No, no, wait a minute," Erika said to Lynn. "I really would like to hear what Harmony has to say. I'm coming from the Dark Ages about all this stuff."

Lynn looked away with an air of strained parental indulgence, wishing she hadn't gone into the Neptune Lounge at all. These rabid feminists bored her silly.

"It's really very simple," Harmony said, leaning on the table, twirling the plastic swizzle stick in her lemonade. "Sexist language is a subliminal way to keep women subjugated to the patriarchy. We're sick of it, that's all," she explained with a friendly smile.

"Like a protest or a reminder?" Erika asked, obviously keenly interested.

"It's more important than that," Harmony asserted, her dark red ponytail swinging with her head's movement.

"Right on," a woman at the bar encouraged. By then, nearly everyone in the lounge – feminist or not – was listening in on the education Erika was receiving.

"Language has to be changed to acknowledge our equality. When you say 'chairman,' you're accepting the concept that only a man could hold that office. It's just as easy to change the title to director, which has no sexist connotations, and allows that either gender is capable of holding the job."

"Oh please," Lynn droned. "Next we'll be changing 'heroine' to 'menoine' or 'heresy' to 'himesy'! The point is that the words you people want to alter have no etymological connection with the male species. 'History' comes from the Greek *histōr*, referring to knowing or being learned. To change it to 'herstory' is ridiculous."

Erika glanced at her briefly, surprised at the young woman's erudition. "Still, Harmony has a good point. If another word can be used that doesn't exclude women . . . why not?"

Harmony glanced incredulously at Lynn but turned a smiling approval on Erika. "Exactly."

"Although," Erika added speculatively, "as a writer, I think some words work better than others. Let's face it . . . a girl is not a woman, and being a woman doesn't make you a lady. There are distinctions that must be observed."

"Right," a woman from the next table affirmed.

"Granted," Harmony conceded affably. "But the practice of men referring to *all* women as girls is unacceptable. It's the same, in theory, as white people calling all black males – no matter how old they are – 'boy.' It's demeaning."

"I'll drink to that," someone said, laughing.

"You'll drink to anything," another voice commented good-naturedly.

"All I'm saying," Harmony resumed, "is what women in the Movement have been saying for years: Acknowledge our existence! Grammatically, men have dominated the language as if only they counted. What's wrong with 'humankind' instead of 'mankind,' or using the plural to avoid sentences like 'A person could never find *his* way'? If you change that to 'People will never find *their* way,' then women aren't excluded."

"Oh bullshit," someone at the bar exclaimed. "You're making it sound as if men had done that intentionally – it's just the way the language evolved."

Harmony glanced up in the direction the voice had come from, then smiled impishly. "True, but it couldn't have evolved that way if women had always been the equals of men. It's time to rectify the error. And see?

Even with swearwords we lose out . . . why can't we say 'cowshit'?"

Erika laughed. "That's one place I'd just as soon let the men take the burden."

"It's one of the reasons," one of the younger women at the bar chimed in, "that we don't want to wear makeup, or high heels, or frilly clothes. We're done up like mannequins of male expectations – throwing our backs out of place with too high heels, squeezing our feet miserably into 'fashionable' shoes – all designed by men. The patriarchy has brainwashed women with costumes that appeal to them . . . not to us. And makeup is just an extension of it. They've got us in 'uniform' to be graded between one and ten, and we're sick of it."

Erika listened carefully, not quite ready to concede the point but willing to consider it with an open mind.

Harmony looked at Erika as if to assess the impact of the woman's explanation. "If we refuse the 'uniform,' " she said, with a kindly tutor's encouragement, "then we are free from the role men assign us." She laughed lightly. "It's one of the reasons I refused to learn how to type or take shorthand in school . . . you can't expect me to do something I never learned. Right?"

Lynn groaned quietly. "Wait a minute," she began tautly, gazing about at the faces and bodies that surrounded her. "If I told you that you could have a face-lift and body correction, absolutely free of charge and guaranteed painless . . . who would any of you want to look like?"

The women exchanged glances, some thoughtfully and others apparently stumped for an answer. "Farrah Fawcett," one said, giggling. "Greta Garbo." A few other famous women's names were tossed in. Nodding, Lynn said: "That's what I thought. You're all just kidding yourselves. Given the chance to be beautiful, outstanding . . . you'd grab it! I think you're just afraid to compete, that's all. What's wrong with looking as nice as you possibly can? Makeup and clothes are to enhance . . . not to hide."

Listening to Lynn with a guarded expression, Harmony heard her out politely. "We don't agree, Lynn. Most of us don't want to look like anyone other than ourselves. Our stance is that men have put us into the position of having to vie for their attention. In brief, we're set up to resent one another in the competition for the Big Prize – men . . . more accurately, a husband. And we don't want that. We want to be accepted as we are, without adornment."

"Nonsense," Lynn protested. "Since recorded times, Homo-sapiens have adorned themselves and painted their faces . . . men as well as women. It's human nature to want to look more attractive than others. Who grows up saying: 'I sure hope I'll be ugly when I'm an adult'? No one!"

Harmony's smile told volumes. "And do you prefer the life of hoping you're never seen without makeup or your hair in curlers? I don't care if a woman is straight or not, we don't want to be loved because of our appearance, but because of who we are."

"Yeah? Well, what about in nature? Why is it that the male birds are more colorful and beautiful than the females?" someone asked.

Looking directly into Erika's questioning gray eyes, Harmony replied evenly: "To a blind person, they are equally beautiful. It's only our conditioning that makes us believe one is more attractive than another."

Lynn leaned toward Erika and gave her a seductive look. "I think I'll toddle along," she said invitingly. "My idea of fun doesn't include a 'cow session' with a bunch of militants."

Nodding, Erika said: "At your age, this is probably old hat. It's one of the problems of getting older. Most of your friends are all in the same age bracket, talk about the same things – you don't have a chance to learn anything new or get the thinking of youth. I'm so far out of things that it's all new to me."

"I'm sure it is," Lynn answered with mock petulance. "What a shame, though, that a perfectly lovely afternoon – when you're free from your friend for a few hours – has to be spent like this. I'd hoped for something quite different when I ran into you here," she stated provocatively. But inside, Lynn was seething. *How can an attractive, intelligent woman like Erika spend her rare moments of free time with these fanatics when she might have had the hours with me?* The possibility that Erika wasn't in the least attracted to her entered Lynn's head, but she dismissed the notion immediately.

Still, once out on the Promenade Deck, Lynn couldn't quite shake that possibility. No one – but *no* one! – had ever failed to find her desirable . . . unless she counted totally straight women. And at that, Lynn was confident that any of those women could have been turned on with very little effort. Youth and beauty were everything in today's world. Why, Lynn knew people who wouldn't dream of inviting someone to their homes who was even five pounds overweight. People couldn't help getting older, but that was no reason for them to let themselves become ugly, offensive to the eyes of onlookers. When people topped thirty, they should join gyms and work out every day; and with the advances in cosmetic surgery, there was never an excuse for wrinkles! Obviously, most people simply had no self-respect. Even that Marsha Whatsherface . . . she could have had a surgical implant at the time her breast was removed. She didn't *have* to go around with that "brave front." And she'd been so irritatingly grateful after they'd had sex – it was pathetic, yet totally unnecessary. If Marsha cared about herself, she'd do something besides wearing a prosthesis. But then, Lynn had to admit she never could understand the way most people's minds worked. If someone was fat, he should diet. Derisively, Lynn reminded herself: *No,* they *should diet.*

She leaned her elbows on the ship's railing, gazing out the starboard side. People were strange, and that was all there was to it. Lesbians in particular. They rarely had any style whatsoever. How much trouble was it to wear a little makeup? To buy clothes that flattered the figure instead of hiding it . . . or worse, wearing clinging cotton tee-shirts that revealed every ounce of flab. Didn't they have any pride? Or were they merely blind to their own bulging ugliness. . . .

"Uh, hi, Lynn."

She turned her head, annoyed with the interruption of her thoughts. "Oh, hello, Julia" She searched to recall the young woman's last name, but failed.

Julia's gummy smile faded as if sensing that her intrusion was unwelcome. "I was just taking a walk. This whole ship would fit on my mom's vegetable garden . . . not much room to exercise."

"Guess not," Lynn responded absently, looking out to sea again, wishing that dreary little person would keep right on going.

"Buy you a drink?" Julia asked uncertainly.

Lynn arched her neck, raising her face to the sky as if supplicating for mercy. "Not on your life! They're all in there arguing inanities."

Julia looked confused, but rallied. "Uh, well, it doesn't have to be on this deck. We could go to the Acapulco Club below."

"I don't think so," Lynn said, still unable to shake off the realization that Erika had preferred to talk to those fools instead of being with her. Yet, Lynn knew that Erika found her attractive; the way the older woman looked at her was a dead giveaway. What had transpired at the Neptune Lounge rattled Lynn, made her question her unchallenged appeal, and she didn't like it.

"Guess you're sort of feeling antisocial, huh?"

Lynn sighed heavily. "I came on this cruise to have a getaway with sun and good times. And what do I get instead? Neo-political gurus, deadbeats, and a lot of terribly declassé stompers."

Julia whistled lightly. "Mad as all that, huh? Well, I kind of agree with you. Not much we can do about it, I reckon."

Lynn faced her, assessing Julia shrewdly. She watched as Julia's eyes roamed down her body, her tongue moistening her lips hungrily. Well, why not? That would certainly show Erika what she'd missed! "Tell you what," she said with sudden sweetness. "Why don't we go to my cabin and have a drink there?"

"Y-your c-cabin?"

"Sure. Just the two of us. You can tell me more about Pumpville."

Obviously flattered but caught offguard, Julia faltered. "Y-you remember where I come f-from?"

Lynn bestowed an ingratiating smile, then linked her arm through Julia's. "Of course. Besides, I'd like to atone for my behavior the other day."

"B-behavior?"

Lynn's hand slid down Julia's arm to clasp her palm. It was moist with nervousness, but Lynn hid her amusement. "Yes, I was terribly rude."

"Y-you were?" Julia allowed herself to be led across the deck toward the passageway that housed the elevator.

"I've a first-class cabin," Lynn crooned, "despite that Carmen woman saying this is a uni-class cruise. The cabins certainly aren't. What deck are you on?" she inquired brightly.

"Fifth," Julia replied tightly, as if Lynn were making idle conversation while accompanying her to the gas chamber. "You sure change moods pretty fast," she remarked.

Lynn laughed gaily. "This is my vacation . . . why should I let those militant people ruin my cruise?"

"Uh, no reason, I guess."

"Of course not," Lynn agreed soothingly as they reached the elevator. *The poor stupid bitch doesn't even know if I plan to give her a drink, bed her, or chop her up with the ship's axe.* Then, as they stepped into the car, she had to silently laugh again. *And that's fair*, she told herself. *I don't know either!* But just as the doors slowly closed, Erika came into view. The look in her eyes was of considerable satisfaction to Lynn – the woman wore an incredulous expression, as if she'd just seen Beauty and the Beast. Smiling to herself, Lynn sidled closer to Julia and raising one eyebrow, waved to Erica, mouthing: "Merry Christmas."

¤ ¤ ¤

A slit of gray was discernible between the swiftly descending mantle of night and the inky depths before her. Felice stood at the prow of Deck 2, where her cabin was, and mused about the events since boarding the S.S. *Sisterhood*. And she thought about Ann. She missed her friend, and it rather surprised Felice. Too, she'd written postcards to all her friends and relatives, planning to mail them tomorrow when they put in at Mazatlán . . . but she hadn't written to Ann. She wondered why. Was there some deep Freudian reason behind the omission? And then she had to laugh at herself. If there was anyone less given to psychological probings and "deep, mysterious urges," Felice couldn't imagine who it might be. She'd long ago accepted that her subconscious was about as beneath the surface as an ice cube in a highball.

The laughter and conversation of passengers reached

her and Felice supposed she was downwind; the cocktail lounge was almost at the center of the deck and the sounds shouldn't have carried that far. Glancing over her shoulder, she noticed a short woman, alone, coming in her direction. Felice knew they'd met the first night of the cruise; she'd seen her about since, and tried to remember her name. Then it came back to her. Charlene McCambridge. She was traveling with that strikingly attractive writer . . . Erika Schultz. On a how-do-you-do, Felice hadn't been particularly impressed with Charlene, but that didn't mean very much.

"Hello," Charlene said as she drew nearer. "Felice Capezio, is that right?"

She smiled. "You've a good memory."

"I'm a literary agent. You have to have that." Her short thick frame leaned back against the railing. "What are you doing all alone out here on such a beautiful night?" she asked.

Felice shrugged. "Trying to decide if I want to catch tonight's movie or dance or what. . . . You?"

Charlene threw her hands in the air. "Cooling off." Seeing Felice's expression of curiosity, she added: "Erika and I just had a terrible argument. Probably one of our worst ever."

"I'm . . . sorry," Felice said, not knowing what else to say.

"I'm so damned sick of her constant excuses for not working!" Then, as if having second thoughts, Charlene looked up at Felice and asked: "Aren't you in publishing?"

"Yes."

The woman brightened perceptibly. "I thought so. Kloberg Publishing, isn't it?"

"Right again."

"It's funny we've never run into each other. I know

just about all the editors there are in New York."

Felice smiled. "I'm not an editor, I'm in permissions."

Charlene's round face fell. "Oh. What a shame. Well," she said all but glancing at her watch, "I'd better be going. I'm to meet Dr. Sue Anthony for a drink. Now, *there*'s an intellectual for you."

"I haven't met her."

Charlene looked her up and down, her lips curling. "No, I suppose you wouldn't."

Too amused to be offended, Felice watched as the stocky woman steered herself in the opposite direction. If the woman had been any more transparent she would've been invisible. But then, it wasn't the first time that someone had assumed Felice to be an editor. It happened all the time in New York, as if publishing had no other employees besides editors and subsidiary rights directors. Writers, agents, or just the snobs, would amble up to Felice at parties, thinking she was "someone," and then get away as quickly as possible after learning she wasn't "important." It didn't bother Felice. It was their problem.

She wondered about Erika. Not that Felice knew many writers – she didn't – but the woman simply didn't strike her as the type. She struck Felice as more of an outdoors person, someone active and on the go. Obviously, Felice acknowledged, she was wrong. Unless, of course, that Charlene had pushed Erika into a career she didn't want. Which, she told herself, would certainly account for their argument that evening. Why did people always try to change others into something they're not? It was such a waste of time . . . a carrot would never be a fig, and vice-versa.

⌑ ⌑ ⌑

That evening, Carmen drew a deep breath outside of Captain Margolies's quarters. She didn't need a mirror to know that her face was red with fury beneath the dark tan; she just hoped that he hadn't been able to perceive it. Then, not wanting to risk his leaving the cabin and seeing her just standing here, Carmen quickly made her way toward Amanda's office just as the doctor was hanging up the telephone. "Hello," Amanda greeted, peering at Carmen above her brass-rimmed reading glasses. Then, noting the expression on Carmen's face, she said: "Oh-oh. What's wrong now?"

Carmen threw herself onto the chair across the desk. "The ol' buzzard rides again."

Amanda sat down, removing her glasses and setting them to one side. "Margolies?"

"The same."

"Now what?"

Sighing, Carmen brought a hand to her temple, rubbing it gently. "Got an aspirin?"

"Does a carpenter have a saw?" she shot back, getting out of her chair to comply, then quickly filled a paper cup with water. "Here," she said, handing it to her friend. "Now, what's this all about?"

Carmen downed the tablet, grateful for the cool water on her parched throat. "He wants me to rewrite my report on the incident with Nick Spiros."

"The would-be rapist second mate?"

"Right."

"But why?"

Carmen wadded up the cup and made a missing toss at the wastebasket. "He says it's because the report will get Spiros fired, and it's too hard to find good second mates."

"What! But that's absurd . . . the man's a menace to any passenger ship!"

"I know that, and you know that . . . tell the captain."

Standing, Carmen crossed over to the far wall and stared at the chart of human anatomy made by some obscure or long-forgotten person who had as much knowledge of medicine as she had of aerodynamics. Amanda frequently smiled when looking at it, Carmen knew, but today wasn't one of those occasions.

Amanda turned and leveled her dark eyes on Carmen. "What did you say?"

"I tried to reason with him, but you know how far that got me. He smirked and said that I was acting just like a woman . . . personalizing everything."

"That's ridiculous. Being drunk is never any excuse to attack a person, and certainly not to attempt to sexually assault a female passenger."

"Margolies's response was that it's because this is an all-lesbian cruise. Are you ready for that? That if it had been a heterosexual couple, Spiros would never have pulled such a stunt."

"Why? Because a man would have been there to protect her?"

Carmen laughed derisively. "Not even that much logic was brought to it. He said that it's because lesbians are a challenge to men, that he'd warned me this might happen."

Amanda shook her head with obvious disbelief. "What he's really saying is that men have a respect for each other's property. But a single woman is fair game, forcibly or otherwise."

"I tried to point out to him – as tactfully as I could – that if the passenger's sexual orientation was what was turning Spiros on, that he'd have been trying to seduce every woman on board." She arched her brows and rubbed her temple again. "The guy was dead drunk on duty, hostile as all hell, and he grabbed the first woman he saw. He was off base and out of line on every count imaginable, and if I hadn't come along right then, who knows what might have happened. I should've let her lover kick his balls right into his throat!"

"So what are you going to do?" Amanda asked softly.

"What *can* I do? He's the captain of this ship and his word is law. I'll just have to rewrite the report or lose my job."

Amanda nodded compassionately. "Of course. But you've still got an ace up your sleeve, you know."

"I do?"

"Sure. Once we get back to L.A., file an amended report directly to the president of Ammex Lines."

"Margolies will find out about it," Carmen reasoned.

"Yes, but once ashore you're no longer under his command."

Carmen smiled slowly, the throbbing headache receding. "You're a genius, doctor."

Amanda grinned broadly. "I have my good days and my bad."

Just at that moment, both women heard a commotion outside the office and Amanda strode to the door, throwing it open. "What's going on?" she asked one of the excited passengers.

"There's a woman overboard," she replied, then rushed toward the elevator.

Carmen leaped to her feet. "Overboard! Oh God . . . not another catastrophe!"

"C'mon, let's find out."

"I should've gone to work with the civil service," Carmen groaned, following the doctor out to the passageway.

CHAPTER NINE

A CROWD HAD ALREADY gathered on the port side as Carmen reached the area, by then a few steps ahead of Amanda. She quickly noted that one of the ship's officers was already in charge, barking orders to the four crewmen on the Bridge Deck. One of the lifeboats was missing, and two of the seamen were in another.

Then she spied a very worried-looking Felice Capezio near the railing and, forgetting about Amanda for a moment, ran toward her. "What happened?"

Felice rolled her eyes heavenward. "I was below, on the Promenade Deck, just staring out to sea, when all of a sudden this dinghy is being lowered before my eyes! It's enough to make a person swear off booze, I'll tell you!"

"How many were in it?"

"Four. I tried to talk them out of it, but they're either spaced or drunk. There was a lot of whispering and giggling. . . ."

Over the babble of the passengers' voices and the ship's officer calling out instructions, Carmen winced at the sounds of the winches screeching and heavy ropes squealing. "Where the hell's the captain?" she muttered.

"Get these passengers out of here," the officer called to Carmen, then turned to one of the crew. "Get the searchlights on!"

Just then, Captain Margolies showed up at a trot and took command. "Call the bridge and tell them to cut the engines," he told the officer.

"All right, ladies," Carmen said, trying to break up the assembled gawkers and clear the deck. Nodding to Amanda to help her out, she was dimly aware of the two crewmen being lowered in the dinghy. She had no idea what had possessed those crazy women to put themselves out to sea, but Carmen could only hope that they hadn't had time to go very far. A split second later, two arcs began to illuminate the water far below even as she heard the metallic grinding of the helm and the ship's engines cut off.

Fortunately, Felice had overcome her shock enough to realize that she could be helping Carmen. Acting like a sheepherder, Felice was coaxing the onlookers to leave the area much as a Girl Scout leader urges on her charges. Carmen had to smile. Despite what was going on, she was glad that Felice had the intelligence and presence to get the passengers out of the way.

Leaning over the railing, Carmen's eyes strained to pick out even a hint of a dinghy, or – God forbid! – heads bobbing in the obsidian swells. Drunk as they had to be, if one of them fell out of the dinghy . . . would she be able to swim? Would she know how to swim in the first place?

Oh God, oh God!

Moments later, Carmen was dimly aware of a number of passengers – probably the same ones – on the Promenade Deck below; some laughing, some taking bets, and some expressing sincere concern. While she couldn't make out all the words, the tones of voice conveyed the nature of the remarks.

"Any luck so far?"

Carmen turned briefly at the sound of Amanda's deep voice. "No," she answered tightly.

"Did they jump or fall?"

"Neither. They appropriated transportation," Carmen answered, nodding toward the two empty berths. She gestured to Amanda. "Look, the crew's just hitting the water now."

Stretching over the side, Amanda asked: "Any sign of them?"

"I can't see them," she said, intently following the beams of the lights. "If I'd had the sense of a soda cracker, I'd have gone into advertising or become a librarian."

Laughing, Amanda replied: "Come on, Carmen. They haven't had enough time to get very far from the ship."

"How far do you have to be to drown?"

"Look, the captain may be an s.o.b., but he knows what he's doing. He'll get them back safely." She placed a warm hand on Carmen's shoulder. "It's not as if they'd just gone off into the Sahara by themselves."

"If might as well be," she said dejectedly. Then, something caught her eye. "What's that?"

"Where?"

"Over there . . . about forty-five degrees east of the light."

Amanda followed the direction of Carmen's pointing hand, and squinting for a moment, she finally replied: "You're right. It's someone in the water."

"Quick! Tell the captain!"

Scant moments later, the bullhorn blared with the captain's voice as the searchlight picked out the person flailing in the ocean. "Search party to port, search party to port!"

"Can you make out where the lifeboat is?" Carmen asked.

"No," she answered.

"A-*hoy*," one of the crew called to the bobbing passenger, throwing a life preserver to her.

"She can't reach it," Amanda said, a tone of urgency in her voice.

"Even if she could, she's probably too drunk to put it on!"

Silently, the two women stood by the railing, unable to speak. It seemed an interminable length of time for the dinghy to draw close enough for an oar to be extended to the woman. Clad in a sleeveless blouse, bare arms reached for it and even at that distance, Carmen could see that she was clinging to the oar desperately. Then, as if in slow motion, the passenger flopped onto her back, still holding onto the oar, and let herself be dragged toward the small boat . . . laughing. The damned fool was *laughing*!

Suddenly, out of the dark, three voices chimed into the night: "You can't see us . . . but we can see you-u-u-u!"

"Oh God," Carmen whispered. "They think this is all a game! Margolies will have them turned into chopped liver for this!"

"Well, there are maritime regulations," Amanda said in a quieting voice, just as the searchlights began to sweep the water beyond.

Suddenly, out of the dark, three voices chimed into "Rub-a-dub-dub, three dykes in a tub. . . ."

"Oh no," Carmen groaned as the lights picked them up. Arms about each other's shoulders, they were awkwardly trying to do a circle, chanting the variation on the children's rhyme. "They'll capsize for sure!"

"Might sober them up," Amanda pointed out, not bothering to conceal the amusement she felt.

"Sure, *you* can think it's funny . . . but I'll be lucky if the captain doesn't have my ass in a sling over this. I might as well try to get a job on the Orient Express!"

"It's been discontinued," Amanda answered, smiling.

"My luck," Carmen mumbled, watching as the ship's two crewmen reached the lifeboat. One of the youngsters took a wild swing at the sailor trying to get her into the dinghy with her drenched friend, but then lost her balance. He picked her up bodily while the other sailor lashed the two boats together.

"Put me down! Put me down, you . . . you *man*!"

It was amazing how clearly the voice carried over the water, when just below Carmen couldn't make out what was being said. "She's got spunk, I'll give her that."

Amanda laughed. "And she'll be humiliated when she sobers up. To think that she had to be rescued by a mere male," she said, letting the sentence dangle.

Carmen shrugged. "I daresay she doesn't even know that she's been saved from anything. Well, at least the water's warm."

"This could've been a cruise to Anchorage, and then what?"

"I don't want to think about it," Carmen replied, feigning a shiver.

"Well, at least it wasn't the apple of your eye involved," Amanda remarked, moving away from the cruise coordinator.

"Hmm? What? Who do you mean?"

Amanda half turned, her dark eyes level with Carmen's. Her high cheekbones seemed even more pronounced in the artificial light of the Bridge Deck. "The bitch . . . Lynn Adler."

"The . . . *what*?" Despite herself, Carmen could feel her color rising. She'd never heard Amanda use that kind of language before and it shocked her.

Smiling slowly, almost sadly, Amanda said: "I can't help but notice the way you look at her, Carmen. But watch out for Lynn. She's the talk of the whole ship, Carmen. Everyone is well aware of her sexual proclivities and total lack of discretion. She's nothing but trouble."

"I don't know what you're talking about," Carmen answered evasively.

"No?" Amanda shook her head slowly. "Well, then I'd suggest you try to keep your mouth closed whenever you're in the same room with her. Your crush precedes you by several feet."

Dumbfounded, Carmen could merely stare after the woman's retreating figure. Soon, only the sounds of the doctor's footsteps on the deck beyond, leading toward the elevator, were the only proof that Amanda had just been with her. Whatever prompted her to make such an observation? Carmen wondered. However, the captain soon strode toward her even as the crew on deck began to hoist the first dinghy back up. Wisely, the two men had split up and there was one sailor in each boat.

Captain Margolies, apparently satisfied that the operation was going well and the danger past, turned to Carmen. "I want those four in my cabin tomorrow morning at ten o'clock sharp."

For once, she couldn't blame him for the fury in his tone. "They'll be pretty hungover, I think."

"I don't give a damn if they've got seaweed in their brains, Navasky! Ten o'clock, and that's an order!"

"Yes, sir." No, she couldn't really blame him. Not this time. . . .

¤ ¤ ¤

Kellie O'Reilly's All Girl Band, beaming, accepted the

cheers and whistles of the dancers at the end of their version of the AC/DC's "Love At First Feel." Then, with a nod of her head, the bandleader counted down: "Three, four, five, and. . . ." The band broke into a 1950s hully-gully.

Felice, nursing a scotch and water to get her nerve up, watched Margaret Anderson dancing with a young woman who couldn't have been more than nineteen. Laughing, Margaret was obviously teaching her partner the slower – and in a way, more sensual – dance. Somehow, now that Margaret had lost that air of lost kitten huddled in a doorway, she seemed considerably younger than before. White hair or not, she was emanating a kind of inner freedom that went beyond years, beyond appearance. She was having a good time, not caring what anyone else might think. That Margaret was about to be a grandmother had nothing to do with this cruise. She was here to be herself, her *real* self. That she had lived most her life in a closet, a respectable matron until her husband's death two years before . . . well, that was then, and now was now. At least for the duration of this cruise, Felice knew that Margaret was transcending the many, many years of being the devoted wife and dutiful mother of three. A caterpillar becoming a butterfly, Felice thought . . . then corrected herself. That was unfair. There were all kinds of butterflies. To put her heterosexual life on the level of a caterpillar was to deny whatever joys Margaret may have had.

What was it that Margaret had said early on in their acquaintance? Oh yes. "I had a choice to make, Felice, and I made it. I knew perfectly well that I had strong lesbian tendencies . . . but I wasn't up to the ridicule and fear lesbians had to face when I was young. I wanted the security of a husband and a home, the pleasure of bringing my own children into the world."

"Did you ever regret it?" Felice had asked, trying to put herself into the woman's shoes in that era.

Margaret had smiled, a little shyly. "No. My husband was a wonderful man in many ways. That I never tingled when he touched me . . . well, after the first few years, who does anyway? We had respect for each other, and a deep understanding that comes from sharing your lives, watching your children grow. I guess that sounds pretty corny to you. . . ."

It had been the afternoon of their first drink together out by the pool. Felice knew that she liked Margaret, but she was also a little afraid of her. That, however, had been before they'd gone to bed together. "No," she had answered, twirling the cubes in her drink, "not corny. Alien . . . yes," she had added, laughing. "I don't think I could ever have stuck out my marriage, with or without children."

Margaret had nodded understandingly. "You're much younger than I, Felice. Times were very different for me. For one thing, it was a rarity for any woman to have a career. A job, certainly; but not a career. And if you weren't married, there was no question that there had to be something wrong with you. Only ugly women were accepted spinsters."

"So, in other words, it was marriage or be called a queer?"

"Usually. Though a friend of mine had a pretty good comeback to such assumptions. Every time she was asked why she wasn't married, she'd answer: 'My husband died in the war.' " Margaret paused, looking at her questioningly. "I'm referring to World War II, of course."

Felice smiled. "Of course."

"Anyway, that was her contention. That the man she might have fallen in love with and stayed married to had *probably* died in that war . . . she certainly hadn't met anyone suitable since then."

"So did she ever get married?"

"A number of times," Margaret answered, laughing.

"Some people just aren't meant to be married. They change partners the way they switch jobs."

"Well, if we go by the breakup factor among gay people, the chances for success are pretty slim."

"Yes, I took that into consideration too. However, nowadays, that seems to have changed quite a bit."

"And now you're out to explore what you put away for so long?"

Margaret's eyes had twinkled behind an expression of embarrassment. "If I'm not too old. My home in Beverly Hills is pretty empty now that the children have grown up and moved away. I want to find companionship, Felice . . . even, well, even love, if I can."

"And you're no longer worried what people will think?"

She'd lifted one shoulder indifferently. "At my age, living with another woman is either out of economic necessity, or purely for companionship. Very few people think anything other than what they want to . . . it spares them from having to use their brains or test their consciences."

"And what would your children do if they found out . . . or even suspected?"

Margaret had put her drink down carefully, a thoughtful expression on her face. "My son would probably be relieved. I think he's gay. One daughter would never speak to me again, and the other would insist I join the local chapter of NOW . . . she's very involved with women's rights."

"Well, two out of three isn't so bad," Felice had said, trying to make light of the matter.

"No . . . but I worry about that one daughter. She's so tied into The Establishment that she gets no pleasure from living. Hers is a cardboard world, filled with papier-maché emotions and values."

"Can you change her," Felice had asked softly.

She shook her head sadly. "No. I can only hope that

some day, somehow, she'll come to see that there's only one name on a tombstone . . . that to live her life for other people's values and expectations is to, well, not be alive at all."

And now, standing by the bar with the copious fishnets and plastic starfish and sea horses affixed to it, Felice was filled with a strange kind of happiness for the woman. She was quite a dame – in the nice sense of the word, as in a woman of rank or a title conferred for an outstanding contribution. Even the young woman dancing with her seemed to sense this, obviously enjoying herself learning how to do one of the "old" dances. And she wondered if she might be missing anything back in New York. Felice doubted it. On Christmas Day, the streets were nearly deserted. People went home for the holidays – wherever home might be – or they were with friends or family. About the only pedestrians to be seen were the strays, the friendless, on their way to the movies or the theater. Theaters did a volume business on holidays, packed with lonely people who had nowhere else to go. No, Manhattan was no place to be on holidays unless you have a lover and very close friends. And New Year's Eve was the pits . . . the parties and forced gaiety, the tacit order that everyone *will* have a good time. Felice hated the phoniness and had often preferred to spend the occasion in her apartment, alone, going to bed at her usual time. Some of her friends had warned her that she was too much of a loner, or that she took such things far too seriously. But Felice didn't agree. She just couldn't bring herself to the pretense of it all; maybe she was kidding herself, but she didn't think so.

Felice sipped on her drink, thinking it might be fun to cut in, when a very tall, distinguished looking woman crossed the dance floor and did just that. At a nod from the newcomer, the band segued from the tempo of the hully-gully into a waltz. Evidently, Margaret's new dance partner wasn't going to take any chances at being shown up on the floor, so had tipped the bandleader for a slower, more graceful pace. And bless her heart, Margaret was beaming like a schoolgirl, falling into step as if she'd been brought up in the days of Johann Strauss. Felice couldn't help smiling, silently urging: Right on, woman, right on.

"Hey, Fel," Donna hailed, rounding the corner of the horseshoe-shaped bar. "All alone?"

"Just hangin' around," she replied, glad to see the tall parole officer. "Where's Sandy?"

Donna grinned, jerking her head toward the floor. "I can't waltz – never could. For that matter, I'm just a rotten dancer of any kind. Two left feet and knock-kneed to boot."

"Is that a pun?" she asked, glancing down at Donna's Western boots.

Donna grinned affably. "Not intentionally," she answered, then turned her gaze toward the dance floor. "Isn't she pretty out there?"

Felice turned and watched Sandy in the arms of a rather stocky but pleasant looking woman. "She's a dear, Donna. You're very lucky to have found each other."

"I know it," Donna replied evenly, as if afraid her emotion might prove embarrassing.

"Let me buy you a drink," Felice suggested, signaling to the woman behind the bar. "What'll it be?"

"Oh, a beer, I guess."

Nodding, Felice told the bartender they wanted a beer, and a scotch and water; it was only her second drink of the evening, but Felice knew from experience that she was too shy to dance unless she had a couple of drinks in her. It was silly, she knew. She had an excellent sense of rhythm, good coordination, and was really quite a good dancer. Still, Felice had a deep respect for the dance, and there was nothing worse than someone on the floor who was stiff as a corpse trying to look graceful. The mere idea that she might be tense was enough to create the problem

. . . but a few drinks cured it.

When their order arrived, Felice handed the tall glass of frosted beer to Donna. "You're not at all jealous," she observed, touched to see Donna's benign smile as she watched Sandy dancing.

"Jealous? No, I guess not. Not like I think you mean, anyway. If I thought Sandy was flirting, or somebody was trying to put the make on her – well, maybe I would be then."

"But you trust her," Felice said, finishing off the first drink and placing it to one side. She caught a glimpse of Margaret, still in the tall woman's arms as the band moved right on to another waltz. *She's in her element,* Felice thought, almost tearing up at the sight.

". . . It's the foundation of any marriage," Donna was saying. "I've never understood why people get jealous of their lovers. If you can't trust someone, why would you live with her?"

"There are all kinds of jealousy," Felice replied, bringing her full attention back to Donna. "Sometimes it isn't a matter of not trusting your lover so much as it's not trusting the people around her."

Donna took a deep swallow of her beer then smiled. "I don't believe that. I'd trust Sandy on a desert island with any dozen lesbians you'd care to choose. If she had a physical relationship with any of them, I'd know she was either drugged or raped."

Felice's brown eyes looked at her with respectful incredulity. "Nothing and no one could tempt Sandy to stray . . . to even be curious?"

Looking down at her, her face earnest, Donna said: "Not a chance. Sandy and I exchanged vows – she'd never betray me."

"Lots of heterosexual couples take vows too, and if adultery were so rare, it wouldn't be among the Ten Commandments."

"You've never been in love, have you, Fel," Donna said in a statement of candor.

"Well, I'd thought I had," Felice answered, laughing softly.

Donna's grin widened. "Maybe you just thought you were. If it had been the real thing, you'd still be together. It isn't easy to make a marriage work, Fel. There's got to be a lot of give and take."

Her mind racing back to Alegra Morris, Felice lifted one shoulder. "Perhaps you're right. Maybe I was just thinking with my clitoris. Being turned on isn't quite the same thing as being in love."

Donna shoved a loose fist into Felice's arm. "Never thought I'd see the day when I could teach a city slicker anything," she remarked playfully, then downed the rest of her drink as Kellie O'Reilly's All Girl Band broke into a bossanova. "Think maybe I'll cut in," she said. "I'll look like a Brazilian square-dancer, but Sandy won't mind."

"Go ahead," Felice urged, watching Margaret being escorted back to her table. "Maybe I'll do the same."

"The white-haired one you've been watching?" At Felice's nod, Donna frowned slightly. "She's kind of uppity, isn't she?"

"No, not at all."

"She never talks to any of us," Donna pointed out gently.

"Because she doesn't understand you, that's all," Felice responded. "It's not a rejection, Donna – honest. Margaret hasn't learned yet that we're all women, no matter how we dress or act."

"Know something?" Donna countered. "I don't think you did either until this cruise."

Felice had to smile. "You're absolutely right . . . I was afraid of lesbians who were . . . well, shall we say, obvious?"

"And you're not anymore?"

She tucked in her chin with a mock accusatory glance. "Weren't you equally uncomfortable with me before we got to know each other? I'll never forget the expression on your face that day when Sandy suggested we all go into port together. . . ."

Donna glanced down at her boots, a silly grin on her face. "Yeah, you're right. I thought you were strictly the Gold Earring Set, not our kind at all."

"So we've both learned something. Right? And frankly, I don't think it's where each of us was coming from. Not totally, anyway. I don't like everybody equally, and I don't think I ever will."

"Are we expected to like everyone?" Donna asked, an expression of having been misinformed in her light blue eyes.

Felice laughed. "I get that impression occasionally."

¤ ¤ ¤

Adjoining the Fish Net Disco was the Acapulco Club. A women's three-piece band played mostly ballads or similarly unobtrusive background music. There was a small dance floor, but Erika had yet to see anybody on it.

She sat alone, within easy view of the bar and entrance, and thought about liquor. She thought hard about it, and about it being hard. Before her was a brimming gin on the rocks with a lemon twist. Erika had been staring at it, toying with it, moving the glass from here to there, for nearly ten minutes. She hadn't had a real drink in three years – did she have to have this one?

She looked at it intently, at the ice cubes reflecting the subdued lighting with cool, moist invitation. They were like prisms, curiosity-provoking and alluring. And after all, what was gin? A recipe utilizing herbs in the distilling process. Coriander, lemon peel, licorice, juniper, and several other ingredients – health food, if you got right down to it. So it was eighty or eighty-six or one-hundred proof? So? It was still made from all-natural foods, wasn't it?

Erika laughed silently, mirthlessly. Her insides felt as if they'd been wadded into a mesh-wire ball; her chest was leaden, and behind the clear gray eyes, a wall of rage and humiliation threatened to spill over momentarily. *You're useless, Erika! As outmoded and unnecessary as an icepick! Why don't you grow up . . . you'd be better off dead! We'd all be better off if you were dead! Who needs a middle-aged parasite in her life?*

Goddamn Charlene! Goddamn her evil, rotten mind! But it had cut her a lot. No matter how Erika tried to reason, then finally lost her temper, Charlene's words had been like the picador's lance, shoving, stabbing, twisting . . . purposefully manipulated to break down the muscle between the shoulder blades of the bull. Perhaps the bull might look up at his tormentor, fully aware that he could destroy the man and the horse if he had a chance – but impaled by that lance, he was a prisoner. *As am I,* Erika reminded herself. Her thoughts played with the analogy of the bullfight, and it was true. Coming from the darkness of the world of bars, she'd been thrust into the harsh sunlight of a world she was unprepared to exist in. Then drawn out, made to show her good and weak points by those who were far more clever. Her first book had been a game; a cinch to write. And once it had been published, they'd hooked her ego. No, not They. Her. Charlene had. From the moment she'd moved in with the woman, Erika had been toying with death – dazzled or just too dumb to realize what Charlene's capework was leading up to. An artful display to enhance Charlene's self-esteem by bringing Erika to this moment of psychic insecurity . . . teasing, maneuvering, outsmarting – all to destroy Erika.

Her world was as circular and inescapable as the bull-ring. The people she'd met through Charlene were all aliens to her, practically extraterrestial beings compared to the friends Erika had made over the years. Charlene made her feel like a bull in a china shop. No, Erika corrected herself, like a bull in a bullring. Everyone knows the bull won't come out of it alive; it's a foregone conclusion. Only the nobility of the beast, the way it fights for its life, separates the bull from a slab of beef on a platter. But no one ever told the bull that, Erika reflected bitterly. No formal document stating that entering the arena was a suicide agreement – sign here.

Charlene's world was inhabited by people who flapped decorously, whose use of language was deft and beguilingly deceitful. Erika lifted the glassful of gin and turned it slowly in her strong, graceful hands. Then she smiled ruefully. *Olè toro.*

It stung the sides of her mouth and prickled her tongue. The smell was like a perfume that had gone sour, like a rancid tuna can.It sluiced down her throat like liquid razor blades, and was felt no more. Erika waited, still holding the glass like a chalice. Warmth began to radiate to the surface of her body, and she felt a kindly numbing in her cranium. She took another long pull from the drink and set the glass down. Tingling began at the nape of her neck, then suffused the back of her skull. She'd never before noticed the effects of alcohol; she drank till she got high and quit before she got drunk. Simple. And then Erika began to experience the occasional blackout and decided that booze was catching up with her. So she had quit. No problems, no hassles. Just quit. And now she wondered why.

It was almost funny to be so clinical about having a drink, to feel the way it coursed down her arms, relaxed the muscles and brought a sigh to her lips. For a second, Erika played with the idea of getting a pack of cigarettes.

THE CRUISE

What good was a drink without a cigarette? But she decided against it. Nobody yet had connected booze with cancer; and if there was anything Erika dreaded, it was cancer. Everybody had to die eventually; but not like that . . . not like that . . . .

She polished off the gin and signaled the barmaid to bring her another. It was hitting her pretty fast, but Erika didn't care. She wanted to obliterate the argument she'd had with Charlene. For that matter, and better yet, to forget that Charlene ever existed. Useless as an icepick. Erika snorted to herself. But an icepick can be used for other things. It can kill. Now, that's power! And then she smiled. Power. *Charlene has power – I don't. I'm through. Washed up. Dead. Nowhere to be. Nowhere to go. Just breathing. Taking up space.*

"You all right, miss?" the barmaid asked, placing the drink down and picking up the empty glass.

Erika looked up. Young. Maybe all of twenty-five. The world ahead of her. "Yeah, yeah," she answered after a moment. "Just solving the problems of the world," she said genially.

The barmaid smiled. "Let me know when you figure out how to make a month's paycheck last more than two weeks, will you?"

Erika nodded good-humoredly. "Buy you a drink?"

"Oh . . . thanks, but I can't. Company rules."

Well, so much for the ol' pizazz, Erika thought, watching the young woman returning to the bar, pausing at other tables and taking the customers' orders. Twenty years ago, that same barmaid – or her mother – would have risked getting fired to be seen at Erika's table. And if she'd thought that Erika was really, truly interested in her, she'd have quit her job.

Not anymore. Nothing was the same now. Older, but not wiser – and certainly not richer. Downhill. Everything was all downhill. Thump . . . thump . . . thump. The carcass of her being was being dragged down the stairs to the garbage bin of eternity. Goddamn that Charlene!

She glanced about the room, dimly aware of the tropical decor and phony palm trees that dotted the Acapulco Club. Beyond the portholes was the void of night. No skyline, no skyscrapers with lighted windows, no neon signs . . . just black infinity, mutely sullen with the absence of the moon.

A few couples were seated at tables, holding hands, stealing kisses. Elsewhere, foursomes laughed softly or were engaged in serious conversation. The room was fairly empty, which Erika assumed was because of the ship's holiday festivities . . . or maybe they were readying for putting in at Mazatlán in the morning. The band stopped playing and Erika turned to watch them put their instruments on their stands. Nobody noticed. Nobody applauded. The players didn't even seem to expect it. Like good butlers, they were paid to do their jobs yet remain invisible. Butlers. Who had a butler anymore? But Erika could remember when she was the toast of New York, invited to all the parties and chic dinners. She'd made Cholly Knickerbocker's column on more than one occasion; had been photographed entering or leaving the latest "in" restaurant or nightclub . . . twenty years ago.

She hadn't cared then. If anything, it had been more of a nuisance than flattering. She'd been "someone" – and Erika simply hadn't realized it. Even when only thirty-six, Erika had felt that the world would always be hers. Age was something that happened to other people – not to her. Never to her. Being broke was okay; it kept your adrenaline pumped up, made you alert to opportunity. Because Erika never had doubted that she would always, somehow, be on top. Twenty years ago. Then Erika couldn't help a small laugh.

"May I know what's so funny?"

She looked up and saw Lynn Adler, then grinned.

"Hi, Legs. I was just thinking that gin is not a drink for amateurs."

"I thought you didn't drink," Lynn declared lightly, gesturing permission to sit.

"I don't," Erika replied, nodding, and admiring the lithe way Lynn sat down. "That is, except for when I do." She suddenly thought that Lynn was like an onion; delicious to eat, but with a definite chance of being repeated over and over. Then she wondered if she was getting drunk. How could she possibly compare the woman to an onion?

"Where's Whatsherface?"

"Hmm? Oh, around somewhere – plying her trade with a self-fornicating Ph.D."

Lynn smiled. "Self-fornicating? Do you mean masturbating?"

Erika shook her head slowly. "No. There's dignity to masturbation. Fornication is abusive."

Lynn looked at her folded hands with shy reserve. "Are you . . . jealous?"

"What?" Erika burst out into a hearty laugh. "Hell, no! They should devour each other like an orgasmic quicksand!"

"Never to be seen or heard from again?" Lynn asked, a small smile on her perfectly outlined lips. "Like falling into some cosmic black hole?"

Erika laughed again, the aptness of the phrase not eluding her. "What'll you have to drink?"

"White wine?"

"Not on your life! This is my first drink in years, and I intend to get good and happy drunk. I'll not drink with anyone who isn't with me."

"Like D'Artagnan?"

"Who?"

"The hero in 'The Three Musketeers.' "

"Never met the guy," Erika replied indifferently, hailing the barmaid over. "Now, what'll it be?"

"Umm . . . a gimlet."

"Gimlet! That's kid stuff, and it'll make you sick as all hell in the morning."

Lynn laughed musically, tossing her shoulder-length hair with practiced ease. "All right, then, a martini." She raised her chin, peered at the young waitress through carefully placed lashes. "Vodka, with an olive."

Somehow, as if in a frozen time-zone, Erika consumed four more gins on the rocks. Lynn sat across from her, smiling and casting seductive green-eyed glances, and all the rest of the room was as if seen through the wrong end of binoculars. The band had come back on, gone off again, and returned . . . how many times? Who knew and who cared? Lynn was the most beautiful woman aboard the S.S. *Sisterhood*, matching her drink for drink, tantalizingly close. So young,so warm, so soft. . . . Her head felt as if someone had put a fur coat around her brain, and Erika was blissfully happy.

". . . Don't be stubborn now."

Erika smiled amiably at Lynn. "Stubborn about what?" At least she wasn't slurring. Erika was sure of that.

"You're getting drunk, Rick. Let me take you to my cabin so you can sleep it off before Mashed Potatoes gives you hell."

"Mashed potatoes," Erika repeated carefully, then laughed. "Yeah . . . I like it. Fits her to a tee. But I thought you wanted me to read some of your writing."

"Will it make any sense to you?"

"Sure! What do you take me for?" She rose to her feet, resting one palm on the table and hoping her unsteadiness wasn't too obvious.

"Shall I help you?" Lynn asked sympathetically.

"No, just point me in the right direction and I'll lurch my way like a goat in a mudslide." Then she roared at her own joke till she felt Lynn's arm about her waist, the nearness of her, the taunting aroma of her perfume.

Moments later, Lynn was closing her stateroom door, and Erika sank onto a burnt-orange sofa. "Anything to drink?"

"Don't you think you've had enough?"

"What I've had enough of isn't in this room," Erika replied with pleased smugness. "Now, c'mon. Get me some of your writing, and if you've any gin or vodka, let's have some."

"Yes, ma'am, right away," Lynn shot back, laughing.

Erika stretched out on the couch, mindful to remain in an upright position lest the gin take her down the whirlpool. When Lynn returned, she had a round tray with a small ice bucket, two drinks already poured, and some typewritten pages propped in between. Setting down the tray, she lifted the paper and slowly rolled it up.

"Are you sure you want to read this now?" She sat down on the edge of the couch next to Erika's hip, then slowly began to unbutton her blouse. Leaning forward, her green eyes darkly glowing, she asked: "Can't you think of anything better to do?"

Erika stifled the groan in her throat, not wanting her hunger for the woman to show through. Slowly, she raised one hand to the full mound of flesh just below Lynn's collarbone. "Are you . . . sure?"

Lynn's eyes became opals of desire. "Yes, but. . . ."

"But?" Erika's hand brushed across Lynn's shoulder with the gentleness of a dissipating dandelion, then back up to stroke her lovely neck.

"I . . . I've never done this before. You'll have to teach me . . . be gentle. . . . "

Erika's head began to pound as Lynn lowered her face to meet hers, lips wet and parted. "You've come to the right department," Erika managed to say just as Lynn's breasts meshed with hers, and their tongues explored tentatively, hotly. . . .

CHAPTER TEN

SANDY AND DONNA STOOD atop El Mirador and gazed out across Mazatlán, and beyond to the incredibly blue Pacific, dotted with sailboats and catamarans. Other tourists had also scaled the towering stone edifice, taking snapshots. "It sure is different than Ensenada," Sandy remarked with hushed awe.

"I could live here," Donna said, about to put her arm around Sandy's waist, then catching herself as she remembered that they weren't on board ship any longer – they were surrounded by straight people, and she'd have to remember that.

"Could you?" Sandy asked, turning to look up. Then she smiled broadly. "Yes, I can see you living here. You'd be out fishing every morning, or taking long walks along the beach. You'd come home with every stray dog for miles around, and then somehow get the local people to throw a fiesta to find them homes."

Donna grinned. "Sounds pretty good to me. Perfect temperature all year long, no smog, plenty of places to go and things to do. Yeah, I sure could live here all right."

"Cost of living's probably less, too," Sandy said, then slipped her hand into Donna's.

Shaking her head, Donna tried to disengage herself, jerking her chin toward the others on the rampart.

"I don't care," Sandy whispered mischievously. "C'mon, let's go down and find the marketplace. I'm so hungry I could eat your boots!"

"I hear they've got a great arts and crafts center here. Sure would like to see what they've got."

"Well, we've two whole days, darling. We'll do anything you want . . . but let's eat first."

"Mexican, continental, or American?" Throwing prudence over her shoulder, Donna brought Sandy's hand up and looped her arm through.

"Anything that's local and genuine. Maybe we'll find a stand at the marketplace. And I'm not going to be happy till we've had some fresh papaya and mango."

They headed down the long, steep ramp arm in arm, the sun beating down on their uncovered heads, and Donna felt an exhilaration she didn't quite understand. Yes, sure, it was good to be away on holiday; and of course, nice to be on shore for a change. But it was more than that. There was something about the place that had captivated her . . . the combination of Old World and New, the sense of freedom the clean air and sea breezes gave her. It was, well, sort of as if maybe she had lived here in a former life and only now had come home again. It was certainly the first time she'd ever contemplated retiring anywhere that wasn't the desert. Yet, there was something special about Mazatlán . . . something even magical. A feeling of timelessness or a tropical Garden of Eden. Lush vegetation, a sheltered harbor glittering in the sunlight – yes, Donna knew she would be very happy to retire to this beautiful place. And either she'd read it somewhere, or maybe Carmen Navasky had mentioned it, but Donna knew that Mazatlán had more trailer parks than any other city in Mexico. They could save up for that Winnebago, come down on vacations, make friends . . . and one day live out the rest of their lives, growing old together, watching the perfect sunsets knowing that all's right with the world. It was a nice dream, and Donna knew that it wasn't impossible. Sandy had already shown that she was delighted with the place; besides, Sandy would never deny her any wish unless it was absolutely crazy.

They strolled casually till they found themselves in the center of town, at the juncture of Zaragoza and Juárez Streets. Inquiring of a passerby, they learned that the marketplace was straight down Calle Juárez, just past Calle Ocampo. They'd already passed several restaurants, but Sandy was adamant about wanting only local food. However, shortly before they reached the market, Donna's glance caught sight of Barbara, Mac, and Carol on the other side of the street. "C'mon, hon, let's hurry."

Sandy looked up, smiling. "Has the hunger bug got you too?"

"Yeah, something like that," Donna fibbed, observing the other three pausing to look at a shop's window display. With any luck at all, she and Sandy could be out of view before they looked up – or worse, looked around and spotted them. Donna had no wish to have to pretend to be friendly with Carol; and if she didn't, then Sandy would become suspicious. And if Sandy learned the turth, well, it could easily ruin their whole vacation.

Sandy stopped walking, then extended her arm. "Oh look! Across the street. . . ."

Donna's blood froze.

"Isn't that that Charlene woman we met the first night out?"

Silently, Donna exhaled heavily, following the direction of Sandy's arm. Squinting, she saw the short, stocky blonde with the out-of-date hairstyle. "Yeah, I think it is. C'mon, I thought you were hungry."

"I am," Sandy responded cheerfully. "It just struck me as sort of weird to be in a totally strange place and see somebody I've met."

Donna smiled but made no reply. She was more concerned about getting them off the street and into the market, going in the opposite direction of Carol – forever, if possible. The vicious little liar. *Little!* Donna tried to keep a straight face. But soon they were inside the market with its many stalls, and safely out of sight.

The aromas and colorful displays of produce, meats, baked goods, and snack stands all blended with appetizing temptation, but it wasn't till they reached a stall selling fresh seafood that Sandy became elated. "Look, darling! Look at that array! It all looks good enough to eat raw!"

And indeed it did. Marlin, sailfish, sea bass, tuna, shrimp, and red snapper . . . just about any kind of creature from the sea or bay was represented with glistening freshness. "There's got to be a stall nearby that sells cooked fish," Donna said.

"I'm drooling," Sandy declared with a little laugh.

"*Camarones . . . pescado. . . .*"

Donna remembered enough from her high-school Spanish to head Sandy in the direction of the female vendor's voice. They found her with a makeshift woodstove and grill, steaming vats surrounded by bay lobsters wriggling on beds of cracked ice and seaweed. A huge earthenware bowl contained previously prepared batter, and the short, chubby woman was literally surrounded with the morning's catch. "I'll bet her husband and sons caught all that," Donna said, feeling like Bojangles at suppertime, her nostrils assailed by the tantalizing smells.

"*Bueno*?" The woman's weathered face broke into an anticipating smile.

Beaming, Donna looked down at Sandy. "What'll it be?"

"Are you kidding? Shrimp!"

Donna swallowed hard. "Uh, *dos* – uh, *cam-ar-on-es*." She gesticulated with an eating motion, knowing full well that her Spanish left a great deal to be desired.

"*Algo más? Unas patatas*?"

Her head bobbing enthusiastically, Donna muttered: "Yeah. That too. Uh, *sí*." She watched as the vendor placed a square of paper, rather like freezer wrap, onto a woven straw plate, then tossed at least two dozen shrimp onto a wooden ladle and lowered them into the bubbling oil for a few seconds only. In another spot, she had a cast-iron frying pan with thinly sliced potatoes frying to a golden brown. The woman handed the two servings across the griddle, and Donna held out her wallet, fishing for singles. "How much? *Cuantos*?"

Nodding pleasantly, the vendor counted off some *centavos* and gave them to Donna, holding up two fingers to indicate that she was giving her the change for two dollars.

That accomplished, Donna scanned the area quickly, looking for someplace to buy a beer. There were flower vendors, fruit stalls, but no place that sold cold beverages. She looked back at the vendor. "*Cerveza*?"

She shook her head. "*Aquí no. Afuera, señorita*."

"What'd she say?" Sandy asked, already munching on one of the fried shrimp. "Umm, these are delicious!"

"Let's go outside. She said something about going outside when I asked about getting a beer."

"Can we take the food with us?"

"I guess so."

"What about her little straw trays?"

Donna shrugged. "Bring them back, I reckon."

"These folks sure are trusting," Sandy commented, laughing. "Let's not worry her, darling. We can eat and then go find the beer afterward. Okay?"

"Sure, I guess so." She lifted one of the fried shrimp to her mouth, expecting it to be greasy. To her surprise, it wasn't; just plump, meaty, and richly succulent. Turning, she noted that Mac, Barbara, and Carol were at the other end of the marketplace, just entering. Donna quickly faced around again, looking for something to block her five-foot-ten frame from their view.

"Donna, what on earth's the matter with you?" Sandy asked with a little frown. "You've been acting as sneaky as Mutt trying to steal Bojangle's dinner!"

"You're imagining things, hon," Donna replied evasively.

"I am not. Just before we got here, you looked as if you'd been caught with your hands in the cookie jar . . . and now you're doing it again."

Donna wolfed down the rest of her lunch. "Let's go find that beer."

Sandy shook her head impatiently. "You're worse than a kid," she admonished, wrapping her food up by the four corners of the paper, and then putting the straw plate back on a stack. "All right, I'll eat as we go along. But I want an explanation, Donna."

"Okay, okay – let's just get out of here."

¤ ¤ ¤

Carmen finished retyping her report on Nick Spiros and put it to one side. It gnawed at her to have to soft-pedal the incident. The new version had all the dramatic effectiveness of a menu. She hated changing "victim" to "subject," or "attacked" to "accosted," yet Margolies had given her no choice. He'd all but dictated how he wanted it to be phrased; but she put the first report into her briefcase and would turn in an amended report once they were back home.

Then she stood and crossed over to the porthole, gazing longingly at the Mazatlán shoreline. It had been almost a year since she'd been there, and she wondered if Mariana still worked at that perfume shop on Calle Vidalmar. Should she go ashore to find out? Then she quickly decided against it. What was over was over. There would be no point to raking up old coals. They'd never really even been friends . . . just lovers. And with that, Carmen thought about Lynn Adler.

She was a strange one, no question about that. And it hadn't escaped her notice that Lynn seemed to single out women who seemed the least likely to be of any interest. Every time Carmen had seen Lynn with someone, the woman was either old, hopelessly awkward or ugly, or in some other way the total antithesis to Lynn herself. Granted, opposites attracted . . . but this seemed to go far deeper than that. Was that why Lynn paid no attention to her? Carmen questioned. Was it her lack of obvious "defect" that left Lynn disinterested? God knew, Carmen had certainly made her own interest in Lynn quite clear to the young woman. Yet Lynn had behaved as if Carmen were invisible. Polite enough; even friendly. But that was all.

Sighing, Carmen went back to her small desk and picked up the report. "May as well take it up to Herr Eichmann," she said softly, amused at her little nickname for him. Hitler's chief administrator for the extermination of the Jews; it was a role she was convinced Margolies would love to have—not for the brutality, but for the supremacy.

Reasonably assured there were few passengers left on the ship, she donned her glasses and stepped out onto the passageway kitty-corner from the Telephone Center on Deck 6. Turning right, just three cabins away, were the two elevators flanked by stairs to above and below decks. She pressed the Up button and waited, tapping the paper against her thigh. When the doors slid open, she wasn't surprised to see that the car was quite empty. Whenever they were in port, Carmen had no difficulty recalling stories of ghosts on abandoned ships; or of voyages peopled by those who had died, didn't know it, and were between this world and the next. An empty ship – which, except for a skeleton crew and the relative handful of passengers, the S.S. *Sisterhood* was at that moment – gave rise to all sorts of eerie speculations.

However, instead of an uninterrupted ascent, the elevator stopped at Deck 4. A disheveled and hung-over Erika Schultz walked in. " 'Morning, Erika. Rough night?"

She smiled sheepishly, running long fingers through her thick hair. "The worst," she admitted in a low voice. "Have you seen Charlene at all?"

"She went ashore . . . maybe two or three hours ago."

"What about Lynn Adler," Erika asked, her eyes half closing as if in great pain.

Carmen kept her expression totally impassive, not wanting Erika to see her surprise. Was that where the woman had spent the night . . . why she was such a wreck? Lynn Adler's cabin was on Deck 4 . . . but then Carmen remembered that Erika and Charlene were also on the same deck. Maybe what she suspected wasn't true after all. "I haven't seen her all morning. Why?"

"Don't ask me any questions, Carmen . . . okay? I'm just not up for it."

Carmen smiled. "Perhaps you need to go off to some mountain to recover."

"I don't think I could stand the rustling of the leaves."

"Oh dear. Bad as all that?"

"If there were a morgue on ship, I'd check in," Erika

said, feebly attempting humor.

"As a matter of fact," Carmen said cheerfully, "all maritime vessels have to carry coffins aboard. Did you know that?"

"No."

"Should anyone die," Carmen went on blithely, "every captain must be prepared."

"That's very interesting," Erika said flatly, resting her forehead against the wall. "Oohh, that feels good."

Carmen laughed. "I think, Ms. Schultz, that you need a hair of the dog."

"Is the bar open?" For a moment, dozens of scenes of "morning after" played across the screen of Erika's mind. Beer, Bloody Mary, screwdriver . . . anything with some alcoholic content had seemed to revive the victim. *Victim*, Erika thought, her forehead in a vise. *So who broke my arm forcing me to have a drink*?

"I'm sure there's someone on duty at the Neptune Lounge . . . some passengers have remained on board, or will come back early. Give it a try." She smiled encouragingly. "Bernie's probably there. She almost never goes ashore."

"Good ol' Bernie," Erika muttered, the sound of her voice reverberating in her head as if she were in the Grand Canyon, then pushed the button for Deck 2, where the promenade was.

Running her hands along the walls of the passageway after she waved good-bye to Carmen, she wondered what Charlene might have thought when she didn't return to their cabin last night. Perhaps she hadn't returned either, and didn't even know . . .?

And where had Lynn gone? She should have been sound asleep, curled up in Erika's arms. Obviously, she had risen early, dressed quietly, and gone off to shore. She tried desperately to recall the night before, but it was all very, very fuzzy. Kissing Lynn, undressing each other, fondling, and . . . and then? Under other circumstances,

Erika might have shaken her head; she wasn't about to risk it now. But at least when she'd returned to her cabin, there'd been no shrieking Charlene, and she'd been able to shower and change clothes in peace. Later? Well, she'd deal with that when the time came.

She rounded the corner and braced herself for the lounge, grateful for the darkened atmosphere, but her stomach rebelling at the odor of stale cigarette smoke and booze. Well, a little drink would take care of that. Why oh why had she been so determined to get drunk? What a stupid, adolescent . . . oh well, it was too late now. *Guilty and alive once more*, Erika told herself with disgusted forgiveness for her weakness.

"Hey, Rick! How're things?"

"Shh," Erika said, sliding her lean torso onto a barstool.

Bernie squinted one eye knowingly. "Comin' right up, ol' buddy," she stated, then asked: "What was it what gotcha?"

"Gin."

Nodding, Bernie lifted out a fifth of gin along with a highball glass. She poured in a substantial amount of the alcohol, cracked a raw egg into it, added celery salt, Tabasco sauce, Worcestershire sauce, and filled the glass to the top with tomato juice. Stirring vigorously, she handed the concoction to Erika. "It'll cure you or kill you."

Erika stared at the dull-red contents, the thought of the raw egg making her queasy. "Are you sure?"

"Never fails," Bernie advised her solemnly. "Go on."

Not wanting to smell the drink, she held her breath and swallowed it in one motion. "Oh man, that's wicked," she gasped. "Don't you need a prescription to make one of these things?"

Bernie grinned. "Now I'll make you a regular Bloody Mary. That should do it."

Erika glanced about the bar with cosmic disinterest. "Guess everyone went ashore."

"No, not everyone. Most, though. Once in port, the ship's like your hotel. Some'll come back for lunch or dinner, an' just 'bout everyone'll come back to sleep."

"Oh."

"There's some kind of meetin' goin' on over at the theater."

"Meeting?"

"Yeah. You know, Women's Lib or somethin'. Sure a lot of 'em on this cruise."

Erika nodded, then quickly stopped when it seemed as if her brains had slid toward her forehead. "Why not?" Then she paused. "Now I remember. It was on the brochures. Something about Consciousness Raising Seminars – I'd just figured it was a lot of Lesbianism 101."

Bernie's mouth turned into a horizontal half moon. " Same thing, isn't it?"

Nursing her drink, Erika was only dimly aware of someone entering the room and didn't answer Bernie. Had it been Princess Di, she couldn't have cared less. Then she was forced to acknowledge the woman's presence as she took the next barstool.

"Ginger ale," the young woman said to Bernie. Clearing her throat, she turned to Erika. "Can I talk to you a second?"

Erika glanced at her without recognition. "Me?"

"Yeah. I, uh, well, I sort of caught a glimpse of you last night – leaving the Acapulco Club with Lynn. Lynn Adler." She smiled nervously, really more on the defensive than belligerent.

Not knowing what this was all about, Erika said nothing.

"I, uh, sort of followed you," she added, her voice breaking with uncertainty.

Glancing toward a discreet Bernie, Erika received no inkling of what the woman wanted. "I'm sorry, I'm afraid –"

"I'm Julia Fee. Cabin 548."

"I still don't –"

"Look, no hard feelings or anything. But I've kind of got Lynn staked out for me – see? She and I have a thing going. It started yesterday afternoon."

Now it all came back to Erika. The woman in the elevator with Lynn. All her alert buttons went on Red. She'd seen some pretty ugly brawls in bars over the years; women breaking beer bottles to use as weapons, slicing up another's face. "I'm sorry, Julia – I didn't know Lynn was 'staked out.' "

"Well, she is. I didn't think you knew. I saw her with a couple of other women, too."

Erika smiled expansively. "Let me buy you a drink, okay?"

"No . . . no, thanks. I don't drink. I just wanted to set the record straight." Julia smiled awkwardly. "No pun intended."

"Well, if she's been with other women too, you can't very well claim you two are an item. No offense, but it sounds more –"

Bernie turned her back on them, polishing a glass while observing Julia in the mirror. Erika was relieved that it was her old chum on duty . . . just in case.

". . . She's just mixed up, that's all," Julia was saying. "She's never been to bed with a woman before, see. I was her first," Julia confided, squaring her shoulders proudly. "She didn't go to bed with those others. And I know she didn't sleep with you either. It's just that I thought you'd like to know that Lynn's trying to find herself."

I've never done this before. You'll have to teach me . . . be gentle. . . . It took all of Erika's reserve not to burst into guffaws in Julia's face. Such a reaction would have been unnecessarily cruel, and that was one thing Erika avoided. It was hard enough to be alive in this damned world without raining on other people's parades! For her own part, the situation didn't matter much. Lynn Adler was beautiful, but Erika's interest in her stopped beyond the idea of bedding her. She was having more trouble than she wanted to think about just having to coexist with Charlene – who needed a psychotic hot-pants to complicate matters? "Well, I'm glad you filled me in, Julia," she said after a moment.

"I thought you'd be," she answered, relaxing somewhat. "Once I get Lynn back to L.A., I'm sure she'll see that we've got something special going."

"I'm sure," Erika said, quickly raising her glass to her full lips. *Poor kid doesn't know what she's let herself in for!* Now that she had a measure of the woman, Erika knew damned well that Lynn wasn't about to tie herself down to any one person. She would doubtlessly work her way through every woman on board; and never remember a one of them. That was all right to Erika. Still, though she hadn't expected her night with Lynn to be anything serious to Lynn, nonetheless Erika also hadn't expected to discover that she'd only been one more notch on the woman's love belt. Erika was rather surprised, but not hurt. Unfortunately, she feared that Julia was in for quite a fall – and Erika didn't want to be anywhere around when Lynn gave her stunned lover the bounce.

". . . I figure we can settle down in Los Angeles. It's far enough from my folks that it shouldn't be a problem."

"Hmm? What?"

"Lynn and me. She's so beautiful yet inexperienced," Julia continued, "that I can hardly believe my good luck. I mean," she said, reddening, "look at me. Next to her,I'm a clod! But I love Lynn, and I'll always take care of her."

Erika looked away quickly, feeling terribly sorry for Julia. "What if Lynn doesn't want to be taken care of?" she asked cautiously, noticing the way Bernie rolled her eyes upward at the question.

Julia laughed uncomfortably. "She does. She just doesn't know it yet. Besides, I'm rich. I can give her anything she wants."

"Maybe she doesn't want that," Erika pointed out, hoping she could at least plant the idea that Julia might not win her ladylove. "Besides, it's a holiday cruise. You know how these shipboard romances are. You two have just barely met – hardly the stuff for enduring, real love."

Julia looked at her as if Erika had taken leave of her senses. "Why, I've been on more cruises than most people take the bus! I know real love when I feel it, Erika. This is it. The woman of my dreams!"

"But what if she doesn't return your feelings – later, I mean, once the cruise is over. Sure, it's all fun and romance now, but –"

"She does. I know she does. And our love will only grow stronger as time goes by!"

Erika sighed inwardly. There was nothing she could say that would dissuade this young woman. Julia would just have to believe the myth of her own creation, and discover on her own that Lynn planned to mash up her heart and spit it out like stale chewing gum – a wad next to hundreds of others. What was the old saying? There are none so blind as those who won't see . . . yes, that was it. And Julia was a classic case. Why did people like Lynn have to exist? She had beauty, style, and obviously, a good education. What joy could there be in leading people like Julia on . . . only to break their hearts, hurting them, perhaps irreparably. Did it make Lynn feel even more desirable? But there was no use speculating on the likes of her. The Lynn Adlers of the world fed upon the fragile egos of others like gypsy moths, oblivious to the swath of destruction they left behind. It wasn't up to Erika to take somebody else's inventory; Julia would just have to take her lumps and learn the hard way.

"Well, I better be on my way," Julia said, sliding

from the stool with a cumbersome motion. "And, thanks, Erika."

"Thanks?"

"Yeah, you really took the news like a champ. I appreciate it."

Erika watched the young woman amble out of the lounge and turning to Bernie, lifted her shoulders helplessly. "I tried."

Bernie's face broke into a lopsided grin. "You sure did, Rick." She leaned on a chrome lever and drew herself a glass of seltzer, then rested her back against the cupboards behind her. "Okay to ask you a personal question?"

"Shoot."

Bernie frowned, causing deep crevices to form on her brow as she toyed with the tips of her red vest. "I've known you one helluva shit-kickin' time, Rick. Right?"

"Right," Erika answered, wondering where this was leading. She was in no frame of mind to reminisce.

"You said the other day that you'd kicked booze. Right?"

"Right. Why?"

"Well, I was just thinkin', that's all. I mean, this hangover you got today. Ain't no way you got that playing Parcheesi. You have to've hung one on pretty good."

Erika looked at her levelly. "That I did."

Bernie studied her with guarded concern. "Somethin' made you fall off the wagon, Rick. Must've been somethin' pretty serious. I seen that broad you're travelin' with – not your style, guy. Not your style at all."

Erika tried to laugh but couldn't.

"So I was thinkin' that maybe you need to talk to somebody. Know what I mean? Somebody what goes way back so you can level."

"Thanks, Bernie, but I don't think so. I just fell off the wagon, that's all. No big deal."

"Hey, I'm a bartender – remember? I've heard 'em all, seen it all. Ain't nothin' new to me, Rick. An' I'd be really honored if I could be of some help." Bernie glanced away self-consciously. "I don't mean to get too nosy or nothin', but if it helps you at all, Rick –"

"Go on," she responded, well aware that Bernie was trying to get something out and was finding it difficult.

"Well, when the passengers come in here, you know I hear what they're talkin' 'bout. Hard to keep secrets on a cruise."

"I know," Erika said quietly.

Bernie looked up apologetically. "They're talkin' 'bout you two like it was a western movie – you're in white, and your girl friend's in black. Nobody likes her, Rick."

Deeply touched by Bernie's obvious loyalty, Erika knew it wouldn't do any good to dump on her old friend. This was a problem she'd just have to work out on her own – somehow, some way. "Thanks, Bernie. You're right, I've a few things to sort through, but nothing I can't handle."

"You sure?"

"Yeah, I'm sure."

"If you change your mind, Rick – well, you know where I am."

Erika grinned feebly, nodded at Bernie, then left the lounge. Once in the fresh air, staring out at Mazatlán nestled at its bay, backed by darkly green mountains, Erika wondered if she should bother to go ashore. Then she decided against it. As cheap as Charlene was, she'd be back on board for lunch, and that would give Erika a chance to find out where she stood with her. It would either be another argument, tight-lipped silence, or with any luck at all, Charlene hadn't even noticed her absence.

Seagulls swooped and their cries pierced the late morning with the urgency of headline news. One spread its wings in a braking sweep and came to settle on the railing about thirty feet from Erika. How nice it must be to be able to fly, Erika thought enviously, then laughed at herself. All it took was money, she reminded herself; for the price of the ticket, she too could "fly" somewhere – anywhere. Spain? Had it changed much? What difference did it make . . . she didn't have the fare anyhow.

Turning, she doubled back to the elevators where there was a diagram of the ship. After a few moments, she located the theater and then waited for the elevator to arrive. . . .

Who knew? Maybe she could use some consciousness raising. At least it was an upward direction – and anything "up" had to be better than where she was right then!

¤ ¤ ¤

The S.S. *Sisterhood*'s passengers were a limited number at lunch and Carmen was just as glad. Rather than serving a complete hot meal, long tables had been set up with a smorgasbord that would amply feed those who chose to come back aboard – or who hadn't left. As usual, when in port, they dispensed with formal seatings since there was no way to predict just how many people would show up.

However, Carmen had noticed that Donna and Sandy had returned to the ship shortly before one o'clock. Probably the only reason Carmen had paid any attention was because the usually happy-looking couple seemed so glum. Whatever had caused it, though, had to have happened while ashore, so it wasn't anything Carmen should concern herself about. For that matter, even happy couples had their fallings out . . . maybe that was what it was. After all, she had her hands full just trying to stay one jump ahead of a shipful of passengers hellbent on having a good time. Carmen was perfectly aware that most of the younger ones were smoking pot. And that was all right with her. In fact, Carmen wished she could get a high out of marijuana; but she couldn't. She was just old enough to prefer liquor, despite the fact that she knew it was worse for her than pot was – although, in the limited quantity that Carmen drank, she doubted it made much difference.

Yet, not to be a spoilsport at the homes of her friends, Carmen had given marijuana and hashish several fair tries. Inevitably, pot made her so sleepy she was boring; and while others were on another plateau, attuned to some deeper significance of the stereo music while smoking hash . . . it invigorated Carmen, wired her, and she would suggest that they all go out someplace. An equally unwelcome response. . . . Besides, there was nothing "romantic" about pot. Carmen wanted to be at some low-lighted restaurant, music playing softly in the background, where she could look into the eyes of another with fascinated anticipation . . . for that, you needed cocktails or wine. Marijuana was for sitting on the floor, wearing an old sweater and jeans; liquor was for sipping, looking especially lovely by candlelight, secure in her own womanliness.

She cast an approving, slightly myopic eye about the dining room on Deck 6. There were about sixty or seventy passengers present, either already at table enjoying lunch, or forming a queue with plates in hand. A decent enough showing to keep the chef relatively happy. Even without her glasses she could recognize most of them.

On the port side of the room, Erika Schultz was seated with Harmony Bourns and some others whom Carmen had met briefly, but hadn't had a chance to get to know. She was happy to see that Erika seemed to have "recovered" from her night's excesses. What she hadn't mentioned to Erika earlier was that Charlene had gone ashore with Dr. Sue Anthony, a cultural anthropologist on faculty at

Columbia in New York City. And Carmen smiled to herself. She hadn't liked Charlene from the beginning, so she was pleased for Erika to be rid of her – even if just briefly. As for the anthropologist, Carmen hadn't spoken with her enough to form any real opinions other than that the woman liked to "hold court," and hated to be interrupted.

Pinky and Olga were seated near the center of the room, laughing with some of their friends. Mac and Carol were not present, though . . . Carmen wondered if they'd run into Donna and Sandy while in town, which might account for the latter couple's dispirited return to the ship.

A quick scan of the dining room showed that Felice Capezio wasn't present, nor her friend, Margaret Anderson. Lynn Adler, of course, was nowhere to be seen since who knew what time that morning.

It was funny about being a cruise coordinator, Carmen reflected. She felt so very responsible for the passengers, doing everything in her power to make them comfortable, hoping they'd all have a good time. She was like that on any cruise; but this one was especially important to her. Carmen wanted these all-lesbian cruises to be a success, to become accepted as a viable aspect of the travel business. There were specially booked cruises for doctors and their families, for teachers, for people wanting to diet and exercise . . . why not for lesbians? The company's second such voyage was scheduled for March, and Carmen was hoping that word of mouth would result in a far stronger showing than this maiden voyage had. Especially if Captain Margolies were to be replaced with someone else. She didn't want him fired; just out of her way. Despite the frustrations and problems of her job, Carmen truly enjoyed every moment of it – usually.

"Carmen?"

She turned and recognized Marsha O'Shea. "Hello there. What can I do for you?"

"I'm not sure," the slightly shorter woman answered.

"I was supposed to meet Lynn Adler today at noon, but I can't find her anywhere."

"Lynn?" A small frown creased her otherwise smooth, tanned brow. "As far as I know, she went ashore . . . well, I didn't actually *see* her leave, but I'm assuming she went into town. Have you tried her cabin?"

Marsha nodded vigorously. "No answer. We made the date a couple of days ago, though. Maybe she forgot."

"Oh," Carmen said sympathetically. "I hope not. Are you sure you didn't get the days or the time mixed up?"

"No, I'm certain," Marsha replied. "Would you forget a date with Lynn?"

"I?" Carmen flushed but tried to laugh it off. "No, I suppose not."

"She promised me that we'd explore the town together and said something about wanting to do some shopping. . . ." Marsha lowered her voice conspiratorially. "She's really very shy, Carmen . . . not that most people would understand that. Lynn's very sensitive and caring. I hate to think of her all alone in a foreign city."

The woman's hazel eyes almost misted with devotion as she spoke about Lynn and Carmen couldn't help wondering just how far their "relationship" had gone. Still, Lynn had been with so many women thus far on the cruise that Carmen couldn't believe any sort of commitment had been made. "You're in love with her, aren't you," she stated quietly.

Marsha bobbed her head. "I'd do *any*thing for her. She's, well, she's just wonderful. Not at all what you'd expect from someone with her looks. She's kind, and . . . and. . . ."

Carmen smiled maternally. "I'm sure she's around somewhere then. Someone all that marvelous wouldn't have forgotten a date, Marsha," she soothed. "Let's both look for her, okay? You take the aft half of the ship, and

I'll take the forward."

"Thanks, Carmen. Gee, thanks!"

She watched Marsha leave the dining room almost at a trot, wondering just how much the woman was reading into their "romance," and how much was real. A more unlikely twosome didn't seem possible, yet. . . . Swallowing her own lascivious thoughts about the high-fashion model, Carmen set off to help find Lynn.

¤ ¤ ¤

"Aw, c'mon, hon. You can't stay mad for the whole cruise. You'll ruin our vacation – and Carol just isn't worth it!"

Sandy, stretched out on the bunk bed, turned from the wall and sat up. Donna had never seen such a glint in Sandy's blue eyes before. It wasn't anger; at least, not the kind Donna was used to. Yet she couldn't quite figure out just what was going through Sandy's head. As it was, Donna was torn between being glad she'd told Sandy the truth, and sorry. It was off her conscience, at least; she'd rarely held anything back from Sandy and it had made her feel guilty ever since that conversation with Carmen, yesterday.

Leveling her gaze at Donna, Sandy sat pertly on the edge of the bunk, her small hands folded on her lap like a schoolgirl. "I don't think you know why I'm upset," she said quietly.

"Because I didn't tell you as soon as I knew," Donna said, not all that certain she was correct.

Sandy shook her head as if Bojangles had just broken a favorite lamp; sadly, yet not really furious with the beast.

"Look, hon, the only reason I didn't tell you was that you'd already had one run-in with Carol. I was afraid you'd take out after her – that's all."

"Oh, Donna," Sandy replied, again shaking her head slowly.

"Well, you know what a hot temper you've got sometimes." She was getting defensive and she knew it. Still, Donna had never seen her like this before and she was confused.

Tears welled up in Sandy's eyes. "I don't know if I'm more upset with myself or with you."

"What do you mean?"

She stood up, her hands still clasped before her, and crossed over to the small writing desk in their cabin. Idly, Sandy opened the center drawer, then closed it. She lifted her chin as if to inspect the ceiling, then sighed slowly. Finally, she turned to face Donna. "Is that how you really think of me?"

"What?" she asked, trying to fathom what might come next.

"Donna, I'm your wife. We're married . . . wedding rings, certificate, and all. But I'm not your reflection . . . you smile, so I do. I'm a whole person."

"Jeez, hon, don't you think I know that?"

"Do you?"

Donna crossed her leg over her knee, wanting to take off her boots but not daring to do anything that might give the impression that she didn't take their conversation seriously. "We've been married for ten years," she answered lamely.

Sandy stood over Donna, a hurt expression on her face. "But you think I haven't changed in all those years. You think I'm exactly the same person I was back then. Why would you leap to the conclusion that I'd just jump on Carol's back and get into some kind of fight?"

Donna was on a little more secure ground then. "Hon, I've known you to do that before," she countered calmly but firmly. "It wouldn't be the first time. Of course, you've been entitled each and every time – don't misunderstand."

She made a pitying laughing sound. "Those times were because I was mad at the very moment, Donna, not thinking about what I was doing. Don't you see that this is different?"

"Different? How?"

Sandy sighed again. "If I'd been right there when Carol had accused you of cheating, then yes, I would've probably gone wild with anger. But to have Carmen come tell you about it, to be nursing that accusation since yesterday, with not a word to me about it . . . that hurts, Donna. It hurts a lot!"

"Gosh, hon, I never meant –"

"No, listen to me," Sandy interrupted. "Husbands and wives have to trust each other. So we're not a man and a woman, but we pledged the same vows just the same. By not telling me what Carmen had said, you're admitting that you don't trust me, or as much as saying that I don't love you enough to bear the problem with you."

Donna scowled. "There was nothing you could do about it, hon. I didn't want to burden you, that's all."

"No, that's not true and you know it. You were *afraid* of what I'd do! Now, *that*'s the truth of it."

Donna was silent a moment, thinking over what Sandy had just said. Then, reflectively, almost apologetically, she said: "I guess maybe you're right. I hadn't thought it through, that's all."

Sandy stepped forward and placed her small hands on either side of Donna's face. "Because you're used to me, Donna. You haven't thought about who I am for one moment . . . I'm still just 'cute little Sandy' to you. No different than the day we met. But I am different . . . so are you. What you did, darling, was to deny me the right to be your partner, your lover."

She pulled Donna's head to her breast and began to

stroke her brushed back, short hair. "You've had a problem, a big one, and shut me out of it. That's not sharing, darling," she chastised gently. "If you'd told me all about it, I could have been helping you through. I know how much that must have hurt you, and I could've helped. But you didn't let me."

Donna fought back the tears that were stinging at her eyes. Sandy was right. She *had* treated her like some irresponsible kid, not giving her the benefit of the doubt. Donna had been terribly unfair, and she hated herself for it. She slipped her arms about Sandy's waist, hugging her tightly. "I'm sorry, hon – honest I am."

"I know you are, darling . . . I know."

"Can you forgive me?"

"On one condition."

Donna looked up, her chest all but bursting with the love she felt for Sandy . . . this new, grown-up person she'd not seen before. It had been her own fault, of course; she had taken Sandy for granted – something she vowed never to do again.

Sandy looked down at her, her blue eyes shining. "I want you to arrange with Carmen that we get to be at the same seating as Carol and Mac. We're going to stare them down, darling. Avoiding those two is just about the same as admitting you're guilty, that Carol was right, and I won't have it."

Donna grinned self-consciously. "I guess I've been pretty cowardly about it."

She smiled lovingly. "We've got to fight fire with fire, and if there's anyone on this ship who's going to be slinking around with tails between their legs, it's not going to be you and me!"

Rising, feeling a swell of pride, thrilling to the feel of diminutive Sandy in her arms, Donna held her close. "I love you – I love you so much that sometimes I can't stand it."

THE CRUISE

¤ ¤ ¤

Felice and Margaret found a charming outdoor restaurant just off the highway that paralleled the ocean. Relieved, they put their assorted parcels and handbags down next to their chairs. "Whew," Margaret exclaimed heavily, slipping off one espadrille. "I don't think there's an inch of this town we haven't covered!"

Smiling despite nagging, tired muscles, Felice said: "There is, but I'll do the rest of it on the back of a burro!" Leaning over to inspect, she asked: "How's your blister?"

"Oh, it'll be all right," Margaret replied. "I should've known better than to wear new shoes to go tramping through town. Now, let's have a closer look at our booty."

"Booty?" Felice laughed.

Margaret shrugged with smiling indifference. "Booty, bounty . . . something like that. I think it comes from the days of the pirates. You know, 'Show me your booty, me fine lad!' "

"Somehow I doubt it," Felice replied, still amused. A pleasant-looking waiter came and took their orders for drinks, then receded. It was such a gloriously beautiful day, Felice thought, marveling at the pendulous, gleaming clouds hovering over the horizon. A tropical paradise if ever she'd seen one; which made her laugh at herself since she'd never been out of the country before.

"Let's see," Margaret said, opening up a small sack. "Silver earrings for No. 1 daughter. . . . You were right, they're perfect for her."

"Where's the poncho we got for your son?"

"Over here." Margaret laughed. "When he gets a load of that pattern and those colors, he'll either know that I've figured out he's gay . . . or he'll wish he had died."

"Oh, I don't think so. He sounds like a pretty level-headed fellow to me. After all, he's got you for a mother," she added sincerely, watching Margaret sort through her purchases, enjoying herself. It was such a pleasure to be in her company, Felice concluded yet again. The woman found delight in everything. No complaining about service, or the quality of food; no sneering about anything . . . just a joy to be with.

"What do you think?" Margaret opened another bag and held up the top half of a native cotton, embroidered shift. "Are you sure it's not too flamboyant for No. 2 daughter?"

The corners of Felice's lips turned down speculatively. "I'd wear it . . . and I'm rather conservative myself."

"You?" Margaret's vivid blue eyes looked at her as if Felice had just confessed to being King Kong in drag. "Not on your life!"

"What do you mean?" she asked, smiling. "Don't you think I'm sort of laid back, unobtrusive . . .?"

Margaret beheld her with mirth-filled eyes and a pursed mouth. "You are a chameleon, Felice. In fact, I would go so far as to say that you are all things to all people."

Cocking her head, Felice asked: "Is that a compliment?" She leaned back as the waiter arrived with their drinks and handed each of them a menu large enough to be a sheriff's notice.

Stretching, Margaret tugged at the fringe of the umbrella and moved it over to block out the sun. "Yes, I suppose so." Then she glanced over at Felice curiously. "Did I embarrass you?"

Felice stirred her Bloody Mary with a dark green plastic palm frond and thought about the question. "A little, I guess. I'm not very accustomed to flattery."

Margaret laughed musically. "You? I should think you'd have heard every seductive phrase known to the human race! Young, lovely, warm, fun. . . ."

Felice stared at the celery stalk in her drink for lack of anything better to do. Try as she did to envision herself the way Margaret was describing, it was impossible.

"You really don't know how wonderful you are, do you," Margaret said after a moment, a look of serious concern on her face.

Looking up, Felice laughed nervously and gave a little shrug.

Sighing lightly, Margaret continued: "Well, perhaps that's all to the good. If you did know, you might be like that manipulative wench, Lynn."

"I'm hardly in her league," Felice said softly.

"Of course not! You're definitely more attractive than she ever hoped to be . . . and you know why? Because you have character and depth, because you don't use your intelligence to belittle or falsely charm . . . that's why! If I had your looks, and were your age, I wouldn't let a day go by that wasn't charmed with at least one very special moment!"

Felice smiled appreciatively, not quite believing her. "Frankly, Margaret, the person you've described is you . . . not me. You're secure, confident, poised. . . ."

Sipping from her drink, Margaret sent her a speculative glance. "Who are you, deep down inside?"

Tilting her head to one side, Felice replied: "The wallflower at her first prom, wearing the dress that was obviously homemade . . . scared silly no one will ever notice her. I'm the one the boy asked to escort only so he shouldn't show up alone . . . but he dances with everyone else." She laughed self-deprecatingly. "Beneath this exterior of Bloomingdale's chic is an acne-covered, insecure teenager."

"Oh my dear Felice," Margaret said comfortingly, her brilliant blue eyes filled with tenderness. "You have so much to offer, yet you're afraid. Don't be. Don't you see how much of life you're missing? You're letting your life be ruled by the little girl you *used* to be . . . not who you are now. There's so little time, Felice . . . so very little.

Don't waste it because you're afraid to be yourself!"

Felice looked at Margaret squarely, filled with admiration. "Margaret?"

Her hand covered Felice's reassuringly. There was nothing sexual to the gesture; merely one woman's genuine compassion for another's feelings. "What is it, Felice?"

"I . . . well, I'm falling in love with you."

Margaret stared at her for a very, very long time.

CHAPTER ELEVEN

BY SIX O'CLOCK, CARMEN noticed that the majority of the passengers had returned to the ship. Some would shower and change before going back to town for dinner at some charming restaurant; and others would prefer to stay aboard. It was a source of never-ending curiosity to Carmen that people would pay good money to take a voyage to foreign places . . . then stay on board when they hit port, or certainly return for all their meals. Granted, some people were purely leery of eating in strange places. Other people were merely too cheap to pay for dinner in a restaurant when it was included in the cost of the tour. But even so. . . . Why fly to Paris if you're not going to get off the airplane? It baffled her, yet she had long since given up trying to understand.

Hurrying to the ship's galley, a huge area forward of the dining room, Carmen had no time to speculate about the vagaries of the human mind. She moved quickly along the passageway until she reached the Tour Desk across from the elevators on Deck 6. Turning at the sound of the doors opening, she was surprised to see Amanda. "Hi. Thought you'd gone into town."

"I did," Amanda said, smiling, then brought her hand out from behind her back. "A present."

Carmen laughed with pleasure. "What a thoughtful thing to do," she exclaimed, delighted with the brilliant red paper flower. Glancing back at Amanda, she noted that the ship's doctor was wearing an absolutely lovely cream-colored lace dress. "You look stunning this evening. Is there a special occasion that I'm not aware of?"

Amanda laughed. "Now, now . . . don't go getting all your panic buttons pushed. I thought it would be fun to dress up even though the captain won't be at the table tonight. That's all." She turned slowly, showing off her dress.

"You've certainly got the figure for it," Carmen admired openly. "And that color against your dark skin is wonderful."

She smiled broadly, her brown eyes gleaming. "Thank you. You know, I think this is the first time you've ever really taken a look at me."

Carmen tried to gloss over the remark. "Well, at least you know I'm not a dirty old woman."

Laughing again, Amanda retorted: "I only know you're not old. Shall we drop it there?"

"Let's do," Carmen quickly agreed, self-consciously.

"Did you get ashore today?" Amanda asked, linking her arm through Carmen's.

Carmen shook her head, embarrassed to tell the truth but too fond of Amanda to lie to her. "No. I spent a goodly part of the afteroon just searching for Lynn Adler." She held up her free hand. "It's not what you think!"

Amanda's face assumed an expression of nun-like amusement. "Did I say anything?"

"Lynn's having some kind of a dalliance with Marsha O'Shea . . . and Marsha had a date with her today. Lynn failed to show up."

Nodding, Amanda remarked: "So of course it was a Red Alert."

"No, not really. I was just trying to be helpful. Poor Marsha's head over heels about Lynn." Sneaking a look at Amanda, Carmen was grateful when she didn't make any comment about her own infatuation with the high-fashion model.

"And did you find her?"

"No. Granted, I didn't search the engine room, but if she's aboard, neither Marsha nor I could locate her. Marsha's a heartbroken wreck."

"In a way, that's probably the kindest awakening she could have had."

Carmen looked at her friend. "Meaning?"

They had reached the door to the galley by then, and Amanda stood a little apart. "Years ago, I was living with a woman and her daughter. I knew I wanted out, but I was afraid of what our breakup would do to my lover and her child."

"That would be tricky," Carmen concurred.

"She had a volatile temper and I was really worried. So I went to see her psychiatrist for advice."

"And he said?"

Amanda smiled. "*She* gave me some advice I've never forgotten." Amanda smoothed the lace on her three-quarter sleeve then looked up at Carmen through dark, curly lashes. "She said that breaking up was a little like knowing you have to bob the tail of a cocker spaniel. Some people might think that it's kinder to the animal to do it in stages, taking a knuckle at a time. But the kindest way of all is to just do it in one fell swoop. Do it, be done with it, and let the other person make her adjustments. To string it out, to have half a relationship, is the cruelest thing of all."

Listening intently, Carmen was keenly aware of the intensity of the woman. "And did you?"

"Yes," Amanda said with a small, wistful smile. "It was, in the long run, far better than dragging out something that was over."

"Is there a moral in this for me?" Carmen inquired hesitantly.

"I don't know, Carmen. If there is, you'll find it." She leaned forward and softly kissed Carmen on the cheek.

Flustered, Carmen smiled uncertainly. "Well, I've really got to get to work. I. . . ."

"Don't let me keep you," Amanda interrupted quietly. "We've plenty of time." She patted Carmen's arm gently, then turned and strolled back toward the elevators.

"Plenty of time?" Carmen repeated aloud. "What on earth does she mean by that?" However, she was certain that it wouldn't be too long before she found out. While Amanda was almost always a step ahead of her, she was never out of calling distance. Then she checked her watch, and Carmen went into the galley. First things first. . . .

¤ ¤ ¤

Erika sauntered away from the ship's theater, her mind aswirl with all the information and exchanges she had heard. It had never entered her head that she had ever, in any way, been a willing accomplice to her own manipulation by others. Especially not by men. And while some of the women at the meeting had been rabidly vituperative, Erika thought differently about it. There had only been a few men who had plainly used her for their selfish advantage; most of them had simply acted out of their own conditioning, never thinking about the consequences. And too, Erika could think of a few women who had also used her to their own gain.

And now that she thought about it, none of these people could have done anything if she hadn't gone along with it. She felt somewhat confused with the barrage of information provided that afternoon. Perhaps, like prostitutes, she had gone along with many arrangements that seemed a fair exchange at the time – but had never considered whether they demeaned or undermined her own self-esteem. It would take time to sort it all out.

Reaching Deck 4, she walked past the Information Desk and turned right onto the passageway that would take her to Cabin 42. Approaching it on her left, she pulled the key from her lightweight jacket, then fitted it into the hole. It turned, but the door wouldn't budge. Surprised, Erika contemplated the door as if only a secret word would open it. It was then that she heard whispers and scuffles from the other side and realized the deadbolt was in place. A cold fury creeped through the marrow of her bones, and her body had become as taut as a cat readying for an attack. *Goddamn her!*

"Charlene! Open this door! I know you're in there!"

More whispers.

Erika began to pound on the door, almost rhythmically. Something akin to primitive instinct told her not to lose her temper, not to lose control, but the rage of years was winning the battle. It was as if she had to see for herself, had to endure the final humiliation. "Open up! Goddamn it, Charlene, I'll bust the door down if you don't!"

Her fist lifting to slam against the door again, it abruptly opened and a woman – that phony Ph.D. – slid past Erika before she had a chance to react. Beyond, Charlene was seated on the edge of her bunk, her chubby shoulders defiantly squared.

THE CRUISE

"Well, *that* was quite a scene," Charlene said, raising her chin haughtily.

Erika stepped into the cabin and her palms grew moist. The room reeked of sex as heavily as musk on a humid night. Silently, she crossed over to her own bunk and threw back the coverlet, then placed her hand on the sheets and pillow. They were still damp from sweat. Somewhere in Erika's head, she could hear growling. "My bed? On *my* bed?"

"I don't know what you're talking about," Charlene answered icily.

Whirling, Erika's features contorted with disgusted disbelief. "You goddamned *cunt*!"

"I won't listen to that kind of language," Charlene responded tightly, getting to her feet. Her hazel eyes had become slits of derision and hostility.

The growling was growing louder and louder. Erika didn't know where it was coming from – somewhere. Inside. No, outside. It suddenly filled the cabin like a cry of a caged beast searching for an exit, a way out, a means back to freedom. Before she knew what she was doing, Erika's arm came up and slapped Charlene across the face, sending the woman sprawling over her bunk. "You know I'm frigid, Erika," she mimicked. "You know I love you, Erika."

"Erika! Please!" Charlene cowered, scrambling as best she could toward the cabin wall, away from Erika. "You don't care about me . . . you never have!"

"That doesn't give you the right to walk on me, Charlene – to treat me like dirt! I tried to love you – but you killed it. I've got feelings, you know," Erika yelled, then went over to the porthole and slammed her palm against it. She could feel the blood pulsing at her temples, at the base of her throat. The taste of bile was putrid in her mouth. The years! All those *years* of living with Charlene!

"Well, now that you've shown your true colors,"

Charlene said huffily, obviously no longer afraid of Erika.

"*My* true colors! You're the cheap slut that would bed a snake if you thought it would do you any good!"

"I refuse to listen to this a second longer."

Erika moved in front of her, blocking her way. "You'll listen, Charlene, until I'm through!"

Her face reddening, Charlene countered tautly: "You're the one who didn't come to bed last night, Erika. Where the hell were *you*? At Sardi's?"

Erika wanted to laugh but couldn't. It was as if all the laughter within her had shriveled, dried to dust with hollow mockery. Shaking her head, Erika replied: "I was with Lynn Adler, that's where."

Charlene drew herself up to her tallest, looking more like a balustrade than a human. "Playing cards, I suppose?"

"Goddamn, but you can be so fucking superior. You and I haven't been to bed together for at least three years. Three, Charlene! Not weeks, not months, but years!"

"So that entitles you to fool around, but not me?"

Erika could feel the anger mounting again and fought to keep control. She stared at Charlene's neck; at the pudgy short neck that could so easily be. . . . No. *No!* Erika strode toward the cabin door and paused momentarily. "I'm through, Charlene. I'm walking out on you."

"Walking out? You? Don't make me laugh!" Charlene's grimace was horrible. "You don't have a dime, Erika. You have nowhere to go but Skid Row." She laughed coldly. "All right . . . go ahead. Go hang around those bums you call friends! But don't come crawling back to me, do you hear?"

A sound like screeching brakes filled Erika's head, and she felt her teeth clench as if glued together. *Kill her! Kill her!* Her heart was beating so furiously that she was surprised her chest wasn't heaving with the force of it. Gripping the side of the door, Erika realized that she wasn't able to focus properly – there was a haze around her, a kind of magnetic field of sheer, utter, all-consuming loathing. *Get out! Get out before you kill her!*

Half running, half stumbling, Erika made her way down the passageway . . . trying to block out the raucous laughter that echoed behind her.

¤ ¤ ¤

Donna and Sandy stood on the Bridge Deck watching the sun as it hovered like a gaudy ballroom chandelier. The bay was calm, mirroring the sky in millions of undulating fragments, and Donna slipped her arm about Sandy's waist. "It just has to be the most beautiful spot in all the world."

"We'll come back, darling. If you love it here that much, we'll just plan to retire here one day."

"What about you? Would you be happy?"

Sandy looked up at her, a wistful smile on her lips. "As long as we have each other, I could be happy in Hell."

Smiling and hugging Sandy closer, she kissed the top of her head. "I'd never ask that of you," Donna teased.

"You wouldn't have to," Sandy replied, leaning her head against Donna's side. "Isn't that what marriage is all about?"

"I think I'm just beginning to learn about that."

Sandy turned and wrapped her arms around Donna's neck. "Did you love the way Carol and Mac left the dining room rather than have dinner with us? I'd have stood up and cheered, except I was worried I'd embarrass you."

Donna laughed. "Nearly did the same thing myself. I feel sorry for Mac, though," she added.

"You needn't bother," Sandy replied. "She's made her bed, let her lie in it!"

"You're usually a lot more charitable than that, hon," Donna remarked, loving the way the late-afternoon sun glinted off Sandy's short light brown hair. About to kiss her, movement caught Donna's eye. Glancing over Sandy's head, she saw Carmen Navasky headed their way and let go of Sandy. By that time, Carmen and they had become quite friendly; mostly, Donna knew, because of Felice. Neither Donna nor Sandy felt uncomfortable with the cruise coordinator any longer. "What's wrong?"

"Have either of you seen Lynn Adler? Ashore or on board?"

Donna and Sandy exchanged looks. "No. Why?"

Carmen looked about as if half expecting to find Lynn lashed to the side of the ship. "Because she seems to be missing. That, or she's cleverly ducked out."

"What?" Sandy asked.

"Marsha O'Shea had a date with her this morning and didn't show up. An hour ago, Julia Fee was all but wringing her hands, saying that she had had a date with Lynn at five . . . but Lynn didn't keep it. Now I've got two nearly hysterical women on my back, neither one knowing about the other, each convinced that something terrible must have happened to Lynn!"

"Do you think something did?" Sandy asked, concerned.

Carmen shrugged. "I give up. I just don't know. Frankly, I don't think Lynn Adler ever intended to keep those dates . . . but I've just got to find her. Let *her* make her excuses . . . lie, if she wants, but having two moon-eyed women nagging at me isn't my idea of fun."

"She struck me as pretty able to take care of herself," Donna said thoughtfully.

Carmen choked back the reply that had come to her lips. Whatever Lynn was up to, her callous behavior had totally cooled Carmen's previous ardor. For whatever Lynn's reasons, she obviously had to play a game of cat and mouse. It wouldn't have surprised Carmen to learn that Lynn had deliberately set the two women up, and purposefully dropped them. It was a shoddy thing to do to anyone . . . but apparently, Lynn didn't care. And of course, Carmen didn't dare reveal the truth to either Marsha or Julia. They would have to find out in their own ways that Lynn was just dangling them for her own amusement.

"C'mon, darling, let's help Carmen find her."

"What? Oh sure. Okay."

¤ ¤ ¤

Felice and Margaret strolled up the gangplank hand in hand. They took the elevator in front of the Tour Desk on Deck 6, and rode up together to Deck 2. Felice's cabin was forward and starboard; Margaret's was the last cabin on the port side, just before the promenade began. Stepping out of the elevator, there was a moment's shyness between them. "Thank you for a wonderful afternoon, Felice. It's probably the most beautiful day of my life . . . I'll never forget it."

Felice's brown eyes took in Margaret tenderly. "Me too."

Margaret's lips parted into a little smile. "You're not hurt or angry?"

"How could I be? Everything you said was true."

"I-I'm very . . . fond of you, Felice. You know that, don't you?"

Nodding, she tried to return the smile. "As long as you haven't closed the door on me, Margaret. If I know I still stand a chance, I'll wait for you to love me, too."

Stepping forward, Margaret embraced Felice, holding her close for a quiet moment. "It's just that I'm so much older than you, Felice. And I have children, a grandchild on the way . . . it wouldn't be fair to you."

"Don't I have anything to say about it?"

Margaret pulled away gently, holding Felice at arm's length. "You have everything to say. I . . . well, I just want us both to be very, very sure. That will take time."

Felice pulled her back into an embrace. "As soon as I get back to New York, I'll sublet my apartment and move to Los Angeles so we can spend every possible moment together. I want to meet your children . . . to be a part of your life."

Margaret shook her head slowly. "It's a typical widow's life, Felice. You'll be bored to death, wondering why you ever thought we might have been happy together. I couldn't bear that. You're only in your mid-thirties . . . you have so very much ahead of you!"

"So do you," Felice answered firmly.

"Time to live?" Margaret smiled ruefully. "Yes, probably. I'm healthy and come from a long line of octogenarians. But in another ten years, I'll be lined, getting old; and in another twenty, I shall very definitely be nothing but an old woman. Then you'll be the age I am now, looking for fun and adventure . . . but tied to a seventy-five-year-old woman, perhaps still healthy and alert, and perhaps not. It frightens me, Felice. It really does."

Felice's soft brown eyes looked at her lovingly. "What makes you think *I'll* live that long? I could be run over by a truck next week, or come down with a crippling illness . . . long before you reach your seventies. Then you'd be stuck with me. . . ."

"It's not likely," Margaret reasoned gently. "I don't give my love lightly, Felice. Once committed, that's it till death do us part. I . . . well, I just can't let myself fall in love with you until I'm sure that you know what you're doing."

Felice smiled. "We'll find out once I've moved to Los Angeles."

"What about your career in New York?"

She laughed. "That's not a career, darling, it's a job. And a job is something I can get anywhere. Don't you see? Since meeting you, coming to know you and respect you, I want more from life. I've only been existing all these years, acting out the routine but never enjoying a moment. I want to wake up in the morning and feel you in my arms. I want to creep out of bed, hating to leave your side . . . yet anxious to begin another day, happy in our love, strong because we are together. You've shown me a whole new way to be, Margaret," she said, holding her closely, feeling a kind of security she'd never dreamed possible. Then Felice felt moisture at her ear and stepped back a pace. "Tears?"

"Of happiness," Margaret said, laughing. "I want to let myself go and love you too, Felice. My instincts say it would be right, that we would never regret it, but. . . ."

"Shh. Let's not think about that. We'll let it happen of its own accord . . . when you're ready. There's no deadline."

Margaret put her forefinger to Felice's lips. "We'll see, Felice. We'll see. . . ."

¤ ¤ ¤

Erika stared at Mazatlán readying for night. Lights began to appear in windows as the sun lowered on the horizon. There was an end-of-the-world surrealism to the vista; as if, once the sun had set, the earth would gradually stop spinning on its axis and then explode, sending bits and pieces into infinity. There would be no traces left; nothing to show that Earth had ever existed, or that a species known as Homo-sapiens had ever evolved. Nothingness. Still, silent, epic nothingness.

How long she'd been standing there, Erika had no

idea. It was as if her life had been put on Hold; except that there was nothing on either end of the line. And there was that word again: Nothing. Zero. Zilch. Naught. Only the gently lapping water against the hull of the ship proved that she was still alive. Where would she go? Where *could* she go? If she'd had any options whatsoever, she would have exercised them long before.

And she looked over the side of the ship; down, down, down to the black-blue of the water, flashing glints of burnt orange occasionally. *It's all over, kid*, she thought, not even surprised that she no longer cared. Somewhere, Erika had read or heard that drowning was the most painless way to die short of slipping away in one's sleep. After the initial struggle to get air into one's lungs, a kind of peaceful tranquility took over – dreamlike, filled with quietude. . . . No more hassles, no more struggle. She found herself smiling bitterly. *What a way to end up!* A bloated corpse washed ashore – no one to recognize her, no one to mourn. Perhaps a few friends in New York would be sorry to learn that she had died; but it would be a brief sorrow. She'd been out of touch for too long; or if she did talk to her old friends, it was always with a happy-go-lucky facade; a pretense that everything in her world was just great. What a farce! What a waste these past six years had been – and now it was too late. It was futile to think she could start anew. She'd been dealt her cards and had played them poorly. Just so many winners per game, lady.

It would be easy. No one would even notice if she went over the side. All she'd have to do is swim toward the horizon; just keep swimming. When she became tired, float on her back for a while, then start swimming again. She would be so far from the ship, or shore, that even if she changed her mind, she'd be too tired to make it back. And then, unable to take another stroke, she would begin to go down. Probably fear, at first. It would be dark by then; no way to see from beneath the surface of the ocean. And Erika nodded. There was no way to see from inside a coffin either. She'd been in a coffin for the past six years – she'd take her chances in the open sea instead.

Slipping out of her shoes, Erika stood poised at the railing. Then she shed her jacket and folded it neatly. She looked up to the sky, noting that the stars were beginning to appear. They were already dead; had died thousands of years ago. The shining lights they sent to earth were nothing more than their emanations still traveling across the light-years, but their sources were long since gone. In a way, Erika felt as if she was in the same situation. Her core, her inner self, was dead; only the waking persona seemed to give off life. It was a lie.

"I think you'll regret it."

Startled, almost frightened, Erika's head turned in the direction of the voice.

Harmony Bourns stepped toward her slowly, carefully. " 'The grave's a fine and private place, but none I think do there embrace.' "

"W-what?" Erika tried to bring her mind back to the present, to the place where Harmony existed.

"Andrew Marvell's poem. Didn't you learn it at college?"

Erika felt as if someone had just dropped a hydrogen bomb, and Harmony was asking her if she had enough light to read by. "I – I didn't go to college."

Harmony was less than a foot away, leaning her arms on the railing, not looking at Erika. "You're either a damned fool, or you didn't hear a word that was said at today's meeting."

"I'm –"

The younger woman smiled enigmatically. "The fight you had with Charlene is common gossip all over the ship, Erika. There's not a woman on board who isn't applauding that you finally told the false Buddha to buzz off."

Erika shook her head as if she had water in her ears.

"Don't you see? You've won! You're free of her! And now you want to kill yourself? Woman, that's crazy."

"I don't think you –"

Harmony turned and grasped Erika by the shoulders. "What is it? You're tapped out? Broke and alone?"

Her shoulders slumping, Erika could only mutely nod.

"Come with us, Erika. Join us. We're growing stronger and we could use your help. You can stay at my place till you get back on your feet, get on top again."

Erika's eyes felt heavy as she looked at Harmony.

She was smiling. "I don't want anything from you, Erika. You're not even my type. I'm just one of thousands of women who want to help other women. We're here for you, expecting nothing in return. You don't have to stay with me, if you're worried about 'complications.' There are plenty of other women willing to give a sister a helping hand. For the first time in history, we've got a network of our own. Come with us . . . start over again."

A second chance? Erika listened to her, but couldn't quite assimilate the information. No strings, no catches, no brass rings – just a second chance. Was it possible? Was it worth trying again? What if . . . what if. . . .

And then Erika began to laugh.

Harmony's eyebrows rose quizzically. "Something funny?"

"Yeah," Erika said, slipping her shoes back on. There was not a way in the world that she'd ever be able to explain it to Harmony – at least, not in the near future. But she'd suddenly remembered what happened in Lynn's cabin last night. She'd fallen asleep while making love to Lynn!

¤ ¤ ¤

THE CRUISE

Donna and Sandy, with Carmen not too far behind, stood in the passageway with perplexed expressions. If Lynn wasn't on this deck, then she simply wasn't on board at all.

Donna stopped, scratching her head while she waited for Carmen to catch up with them. Then she became aware of a kind of moaning from the cabin behind her. Instantly alert, Donna lifted a hushing finger to her lips, gesturing to Sandy to listen.

The moans increased in intensity, like a wounded animal's last gasping pleas. As Carmen approached, Donna took her arm. "Lynn's in there," she whispered, glancing at Sandy with heavy anticipation. "She must be bound and gagged."

Carmen's face became a mask of fear as she strained to hear, and then the moans became unmistakable. "But . . . but that's the captain's cabin. . . ." Her voice trailed off as the awful realization sank in. "Oh God!"

"Shh," Donna admonished. "I'm going in."

Sandy frowned. "Darling, you can't! You're off duty!"

Donna looked down at her, her pale blue eyes clear and sincerely steady. "I can't help that."

Carmen shook her head slowly. "I don't like this," she said in hushed tones. "But what else can we do? If Lynn's in there . . . oh God."

"But what if she isn't?" Sandy asked with simple logic. "I thought captains of ships were the law . . . he could put enough pressure on Donna to get her fired! She'd lose her tenure."

"Hon, I've just got to do it. We can't risk Lynn being – it's too awful. I don't even want to say it."

"We've looked everywhere else," Carmen admitted reluctantly. "But to break down the captain's door!"

A man's high-pitched laughter reached them through the closed door. "That's it, Lynn. Yes! Yes!"

"Hear that?" Donna's jaw jutted out defiantly.

"I can't stand much more of this, Lynn," the captain's strangled voice said loudly.

"*He* can't stand it," Donna echoed with growing outrage. "That's it! I'm going in!"

Carmen nodded. "We're in this together, then. I won't let you take all the blame alone." Even if it cost her her job, there was no way Carmen's conscience could know that Lynn was on the other side of that door, enduring God-knew what abuses at Margolies's hot, sweaty hands, and fail to act. Who knew what he'd already done to her? And Carmen recalled the sidelong glances of lust the captain had sent Lynn's way every time he'd seen her, or they'd been at table. The dirty, rotten. . . .

Donna moved as far away from the captain's door as she could, crouching against the opposite wall, putting her right shoulder forward. Then she lunged with all her might!

Doubting that Donna would be strong enough, Carmen squeezed her eyes shut, fearing that Donna would have to try time and time again . . . and by then, the captain would probably have his gun at the ready. Instead, Carmen heard the crunch of a door giving way and opened her startled eyes.

Donna was getting up from the floor just as Sandy was moving toward the open doorway. "Captain!"

"What the hell is –" He tried to disentangle himself, awkwardly, failing hopelessly.

Carmen's mouth fell agape as she took in the scenario. Lynn Adler was stark naked except for a pair of the captain's jockey shorts and his hat, pulling herself out from beneath a peach-colored peignoir where the captain's erection was swiftly wilting. She appeared utterly unperturbed by the interruption; in fact, she seemed rather smugly indifferent.

However, the captain's face had turned a beet red. His lipstick was smudged slightly, and his large hazel eyes appeared twice their normal size with the mascara and eye shadow. Actually, he was quite beautiful as a woman. . . .

Donna turned to Lynn solicitously. "You all right?"

"I'm having the time of my life," she answered cheerfully. "What's the problem?"

"Out! Goddamn it! All of you – *get out!*" He strode to the closet and pulled on a dark blue robe, turning his back to them.

"Oh, Freddie," Lynn cooed, going to him.

He shoved her aside roughly and glowered at all of them. "One word of this," he hissed, wiping at his face with his sleeve. "One word, and there'll be such a slander suit you'll never know what hit you! Do you hear me?"

"Even me, Freddie? Do I have to go too? Just when we were. . . ." She had managed to pull a blouse and skirt on hastily.

"Out!"

Donna, Sandy, and Carmen filed silently back to the passageway, waiting for a pouting Lynn to join them. Once she was outside of his cabin, Donna made a half-hearted effort to pull the door closed despite its being off one hinge.

"Well! You three certainly have lousy timing! What the hell made you come bursting in like that? Why didn't you just knock? And what business is it of yours anyway?" she added petulantly.

Carmen stepped between Donna and Lynn. "It's a very, very long story, Lynn. I'll take full responsibility for what's happened." Getting no reply from the disheveled – and really not so lovely – model, Carmen continued with greater authority: "You'll find a couple of people have been worried sick about you, Lynn. I'm sure you'll want to tell them you're all right."

Scowling, Lynn Adler turned brusquely. "Bunch of idiot meddlers," she muttered as she hurried away.

"Well," Carmen said, looking from Sandy to Donna. "That takes care of that."

Sandy first, joined by Carmen, began to giggle, then laugh; and by the time they were unable to repress actual guffaws, Donna began to see the humor of the situation. "Well I'll be damned!"

¤ ¤ ¤

On Monday, December 27, as the S.S. *Sisterhood* pulled out of the Mazatlán harbor, Carmen was in the Neptune Lounge about five o'clock. Bernie had everything ready for the rush of passengers at the cocktail hour, but was busily polishing the glasses till they sparkled. At one point, she looked up and noticed that Carmen was watching her. Neither of them said a word; they merely smiled at each other . . . a knowing, caring kind of smile.

A door was thrown open and short, dumpy Charlene McCambridge stomped into the lounge, heading straight toward Carmen. "Do you know where Erika went?" she demanded, the muscles of her thick neck standing out. "She's been gone since yesterday! Isn't your job to keep track of the passengers?"

Carmen glanced up, glad to see that Felice, Margaret, Donna, and Sandy were entering. "I should say that I don't know, but I do."

Just then, Harmony and some of her friends came into the room, taking chairs at tables, or sitting at the bar. There was an electricity in the atmosphere, a charge of solidarity. Seven days before, they were mostly strangers to one another; now they shared a bond.

". . . I demand to know, do you hear me?" Charlene was screaming, her chubby hands balling into fists. "She can't do this to *me*! She's got a contract, an obligation to be met!"

"What makes you think she won't meet it?" Carmen asked softly, a pleasant expression on her face, winking at Harmony.

"Because she's a nothing! She can't function without me!"

Harmony closed her eyes briefly, almost beatifically, then gazed at Charlene. "I think you have it backwards, Charlene. You can't exist without your whipping post . . . and at this moment," she looked at her wristwatch, "Erika's airborne."

"Where!" Charlene shouted, wheeling to face Harmony. A strange kind of maddened panic was on her pasty face.

Harmony smiled secretively. "Where she'll be safe and cared about," she answered cryptically.

Fuming, Charlene stared at her adversary; then slowly, almost as if she were melting, Charlene sank onto a chair. Tears began to stream down her cheeks as her lips quivered. "You mean . . . I'm alone? All alone?"

Felice went to her and helped Charlene to her feet. "I'll take you back to your cabin," she offered.

Carmen was surprised when Charlene made no protest, but simply allowed herself to be led away. "Too bad it wasn't Charlene who got off the ship," she stated quietly when none of the others said anything.

"She probably will once we hit Acapulco," Margaret said.

"I'll drink to that," Donna said, grinning.

"What'll it be?" Bernie asked, her lined face beaming.

Each of them named their drinks, talking animatedly, a sense of relief on the air as if the ship had narrowly averted disaster. *Well,* Carmen thought, *in a way it has.* And then she noticed that Amanda had entered the lounge, a puckish smile on her lips.

Coming over to Carmen, Amanda whispered: "The captain isn't feeling too well this evening . . . said he'd have his meal in his cabin."

"Why do I have this feeling we won't see him again till we return to L.A.?" Carmen inquired with feigned innocence.

Amanda smiled wryly. "Because you're probably right."

"Does everyone aboard know what happened?"

"If they don't, they'd have to be deaf. There isn't a soul who isn't talking about it," Amanda replied. Then becoming slightly more serious, she asked: "What about Lynn?"

"What about her?" Carmen countered playfully.

"She'll be a leper for the rest of this trip, you know that, don't you? There's not a woman on board who's going to speak to her after what's happened."

"That's rather sad," Carmen said genuinely. "After all, it's really none of our business."

Amanda shrugged. "That all depends on one's viewpoint, doesn't it?" Still, she moved closer in an almost proprietary way.

Felice came back into the room, a bittersweet smile on her lips as she stood next to Margaret, holding her hand. "It just doesn't seem right," she said at large. "Someone like Erika, so proud, having to slink off like a puppy with its tail between its legs."

"But she hasn't," Harmony interjected. "She isn't 'running away,' Felice – she's walked out on the past to start a new life. There's a big difference."

Bernie nodded her assent. "I've known Rick a lotta years. Ain't no way she ever ran from nothin'. I've seen her stand up to motorcycle gangs, the Mafia, an' just 'bout any other kind of really rough guys. My Rick ain't doin' no fadeaway." She looked over at Carmen. "Right?"

"You'd know far better than I," the woman responded. "Yet, I can't imagine Erika ever running away. The picture just doesn't fit."

Harmony smiled appreciatively. "What would she have accomplished by staying aboard for the rest of the cruise? More battles with Charlene? More abuse? No. A good general knows when it's wise to retreat in order to remobilize – that's not cowardice, but a life-saving act to win the war." She turned to gaze at Bernie in camaraderie. "Let Charlene stew in the fat of her own sick thoughts."

A murmur of assent went through the lounge just as Bernie held up her hands to silence the group, lifting a glass of seltzer. "To Rick," she said proudly, her eyes glistening. "Here's lookin' at you, kid."

There was a moment's silence, then a loud cheer. Seconds later, it was as if nothing had ever happened. Carmen walked among the passengers, listening to their conversations, enjoying their laughter and happy spirits. The cruise wasn't even halfway over . . . but they'd all learned a great deal. It was a helluva way to start off their first all-lesbian cruise! And then Carmen smiled to herself. Ammex Lines would never know what it had wrought. . . .

"Carmen?"

She turned, half expecting some new disaster when she saw Marsha and Julia standing before her. "Yes?"

"We just wanted to thank you," Marsha said with embarrassment.

"You knew all along, didn't you?" Julia asked. At Carmen's nod, she grinned. "It's okay, don't worry. You'll never know what a favor Lynn did us," she said, putting her arm around Marsha.

"The two of you . . .?" Julia blushed, and Carmen could only shake her head as they headed toward the bar. Yes, it was a helluva way to launch a maiden voyage . . . a helluva way. Soon it would be New Year's Eve; what a party they all would have! Then she felt eyes staring at her and turned. Smiling, she walked toward Amanda, who was holding a martini out to her.

"Long live the S.S. *Sisterhood*," Amanda toasted.

Carmen clinked her glass against Amanda's just as the piped in music began to play "Some Enchanted Evening." She smiled to herself. Each of them had indeed met a stranger aboard and had been changed because of it. "Long live the S.S. *Sisterhood*," Carmen repeated – and she meant it. It was quite a cruise. . . .

THE END

THE COLLECTED WORKS OF PAULA CHRISTIAN

Between 1959 and 1965, Paula Christian was considered one of the top three writers of lesbian fiction. Timely Books has now republished all six of her earlier novels, identically bound in dark blue faux leather, title and author's name gold stamped, in a 5½" x 8½" format.

For further particulars, send a self-addressed, stamped envelope to Timely Books, P.O. Box 267, New Milford, CT 06776.

". . . One of the best lesbian writers I've read in a long time. Even though the novels were written almost twenty years ago, they still have a certain freshness and originality. They are a part of lesbian history."

– *Vickie Markle*, **Fifth Freedom**

"Her persective gives women-identified-women a lot of material to grapple with. If you are a lover of quality lesbian literature, these books are a must. . . ."

– *Catherine Kemmering*, **Gay Community News**